Jerrica made it up to her apartment, got through the triple locks and shut the door behind her.

Her gaze flicked about the room, and a shot of adrenaline lanced her system.

She dropped her dinner, plunged her hand into the front pocket of her backpack and pulled out her .22.

"Get out here with your hands up or I swear to God I'll shoot you through the bathroom wall."

The door to the bathroom inched open and a pair of hands poked through the opening, fingers wiggling. "Don't shoot. I even brought a bottle of wine."

Jerrica lowered her weapon with unsteady hands and closed her eyes as she braced one hand against the wall.

Just like that Gray Prescott had slipped past her best defenses...like he always did.

CODE CONSPIRACY

CAROL ERICSON

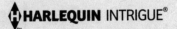

HARLEQUIN INTRIGUE®

Recycling programs
for this product may
not exist in your area.

ISBN-13: 978-1-335-13551-3

Code Conspiracy

Copyright © 2019 by Carol Ericson

HARLEQUIN®
www.Harlequin.com

Printed in U.S.A.

Carol Ericson is a bestselling, award-winning author of more than forty books. She has an eerie fascination for true-crime stories, a love of film noir and a weakness for reality TV, all of which fuel her imagination to create her own tales of murder, mayhem and mystery. To find out more about Carol and her current projects, please visit her website at www.carolericson.com, "where romance flirts with danger."

Books by Carol Ericson

Harlequin Intrigue

Red, White and Built: Delta Force Deliverance

Enemy Infiltration
Undercover Accomplice
Code Conspiracy

Red, White and Built: Pumped Up

Delta Force Defender
Delta Force Daddy
Delta Force Die Hard

Red, White and Built

Locked, Loaded and SEALed
Alpha Bravo SEAL
Bullseye: SEAL
Point Blank SEAL
Secured by the SEAL
Bulletproof SEAL

Her Alibi

Harlequin Intrigue Noir

Toxic

Visit the Author Profile page at Harlequin.com.

CAST OF CHARACTERS

Jerrica West—This computer hacker works for Dreadworm, which is dedicated to a more transparent government, but she has stumbled onto something that's put her life at risk. Now she must work with the Delta Force soldier she once loved and betrayed.

Gray Prescott—In order to clear his commander's name, this Delta Force soldier must join forces with the computer hacker who broke his heart when she broke his trust, but has she changed, or has he?

Olaf—The founder of Dreadworm is either a hero or a villain, depending on what he decides to leak, and he has enough data at his fingertips to help the government or bring it down.

Amit Malhotra—A computer nerd and hacker who doesn't realize the danger of the high-stakes game he's playing...until it's too late.

Major Rex Denver—Framed for working with a terrorist group, the Delta Force commander has gone AWOL and is on the run, but he knows he's onto a larger plot and can count on his squad to have his back and help clear his name.

Prologue

"Dreadworm."

The speaker, slouching behind a post on the tracks of the central Berlin train station, drew out the last syllable of the word and it reverberated in Rex Denver's chest like an omen. He coughed as if to dislodge it from his throat.

"Dreadworm? You mean the hacking group?"

"Only they can break into the CIA's computer system." The man drew the hood of his gray sweatshirt more tightly around his face with a pair of gloved hands. "Rumor has it they've already been successful."

Denver had a side view only, but he didn't care. The identity of the informant held no interest for him, but his words acted like an electric prod.

"You're sure the CIA is behind this setup? In league with an international band of terrorists?" Denver's gut roiled and tumbled, bitter bile clawing its way up his throat.

"The entire Central Intelligence Agency?"

The man jerked his head from side to side, his hood moving with it. "No, but forces within that agency...and others...are actively working against US interests and that means holding the government hostage with the threat of some kind of terrorist attack."

Denver swore and spit the sour taste in his mouth onto the train tracks. "Why are you telling *me* this? Reaching out to me in this secretive way?"

"Call me a concerned citizen."

Denver snorted. "Most concerned citizens don't risk their lives and livelihood on what could be a conspiracy hoax."

"Was the attack on you, your Delta Force teammate and that army ranger a hoax? Is the campaign to discredit you and label you a traitor a hoax?"

"Hell, no. That's real."

"So is this."

"Why not go to the director? I'm just gonna assume here that you're CIA."

"Don't assume anything, Major Denver. I have no solid proof that this is happening." The informant lifted a pair of narrow shoulders. "And I don't know whom to trust."

"The director?" A cold chill seeped into Denver's bones and it had nothing to do with the empty tracks he was straddling in the dank tunnel, his hand flattened against the damp wall.

"It could be anyone. That's why you need Dreadworm. They can cross all boundaries. They *have* crossed all boundaries."

"Their leader, Olaf, is in hiding."

"So are you, Major Denver. Tell me. How did you get from Afghanistan to the streets of Berlin without showing up on anyone's radar?"

"You know that thing you said about trust?" Denver shoved his cold hands into his pockets. "Right about now, I trust no one—except my Delta Force team."

"That's wise. They're the only ones who have been actively working to clear your name…and they're getting close." The man stepped back against the wall as the tracks beneath them vibrated. "You don't have to explain—dark-haired man with a beard slipping across borders with the other refugees. Who would stop to think the mass of people contained an American Delta Force soldier?"

Denver didn't plan to reveal his secrets to anyone—not even a shadow in the night with his *own* secrets. "I know someone who works with Dreadworm."

"Then I suggest you start pulling in favors, major."

The informant stepped forward, and Denver jerked back, gripping the weapon in his pocket.

"Stay where you are."

"Your contacts at Dreadworm might be interested in this." He held up a cardboard wheel in his gloved hand. "Go ahead. Take it."

Denver snatched the circular object and shoved it into his pocket. "I should pass this on to Dreadworm?"

"That would be advisable." The informant pulled the collar of his jacket close around his neck. "Because Dreadworm is your only hope right now. Dreadworm is *our* only hope—I never thought I'd hear myself say those words."

"Wait." Denver peered into the blackness, as the man stepped back. "How am I going to contact you again?"

"I'll find you when I need to." He laughed, a hollow sound that echoed in the tunnel. "After all, we need to save the world."

A light appeared at the end of the tunnel, outlining the slim figure hugging the wall, and Denver prayed it was a metaphor for his current situation. Could Dreadworm really be the light at the end of *his* tunnel?

The shrill train whistle made his teeth ache. Denver climbed off the tracks, his head cranked over his shoulder, his eyeballs throbbing with the effort to pick out his informant, still on the tracks in the path of the oncoming train.

Denver shouted. "Get out of the way!"

The light from the train flooded the tunnel, the empty tunnel, and as Denver stepped back

She'd lost him. Damn, she'd gotten good at losing people.

She threaded her way through the cars back to the sidewalk and slipped down a small alley. Two doors down, she formed a fist and banged on the metal. She had the access card that would gain her entry, but she knew Amit would be working away and she preferred not to surprise him by slipping in unannounced.

He really needed to adjust his schedule every once in a while—predictability could be dangerous in their line of work.

A lock clicked from the inside, and Jerrica eased open the door just widely enough to insert her body through the space. She placed both hands against the cold surface to make sure the door closed with a snap. Then she glanced at the video display above the door—the alley remained empty.

Her heavy boots clomped on the stairs as she made her way up to the work area.

Amit looked up from his computer monitor, adjusting his glasses. "I thought you were coming in earlier."

Jerrica swung her pack from her back and settled into a chair in front of a scrolling display of numbers and letters. "Did Dreadworm turn into a nine-to-five gig while I was busy programming?"

"Don't bite my head off." Amit ducked behind his screen. "I was just asking."

"I think I was being followed." She held her breath, waiting for Amit's outburst.

He sniffed and wiped his nose with a tissue. "What else is new?"

"What's that supposed to mean?" She leveled a finger at the crumpled tissue in his hand. "Do *not* leave that thing lying around. Nobody wants your germs...or your judgment."

"I'm not sick. I have allergies."

"Whatever. I'm getting tired of picking them up."

"All right. All right." Amit stuffed the thing into his front pocket.

She narrowed her eyes. "You didn't answer me. You're not worried that someone was on my tail?"

"You *think* someone was on your tail. When is someone *not* on your tail, Jerrica? Or trying to hack into your computer? Or peeping in your window at night?"

Blinking her lashes, she cocked her head. "They caught onto Olaf, didn't they? Do you want to go into hiding like him? I don't."

Amit slumped in his chair and pushed his glasses to the top of his head, making his hair stick up. "What did you uncover last week that has you looking over your shoulder again?"

"I'm not ready to reveal it yet." She double-clicked on the screen to stop the scrolling and entered another command.

"You don't have to reveal it publicly, but you can tell me, Kiera and Cedar in the other office." He circled his index finger in the air. "We work together. We're coworkers, remember?"

"Coworkers?" She brushed her bangs out of her eyes. "We're hackers. Olaf always wanted us to work on our own stuff. That's why the two of us are here and Kiera and Cedar are…somewhere else. I'll reveal it when I'm ready."

Amit shook his head and attacked his keyboard. "You and Olaf are two of a kind. Do you know where he is?"

"Why would he tell me? Why would he tell anyone? It's safer to keep to yourself." She turned away and stashed her backpack under her desk.

"It might be safer, Jerrica, but there's more to life than safety." His long fingers hovered over the keyboard. "You wanna go to a party tonight with me and Kelly?"

"I have work to do." She batted her lashes at him. "And, as you so kindly pointed out, I came in late."

"I'm going to take off in about two hours. Are you sure you want to stay here by yourself?"

"I thought you weren't concerned about safety? You were here by yourself." She wiggled her fingers above the keys. "Besides, this is one of the most secure places in Manhattan—cameras, locks, motion sensors. I'm good."

"The person supposedly following you didn't see you come into this building, did he?"

"There was no *supposedly* about it, but no, he didn't follow me here. I lost him." She wrinkled her nose. "I gotta get back to what I was working on."

"I can take a hint."

The steady clicking from Amit's keyboard indicated a dogged determination and concerted commitment. Amit might pretend that it was Jerrica who was the obsessed one, but the fire blazed in his gut just as hotly as it did in hers.

They each had their own reasons for their dedication to hacking into government systems and exposing the lies and corruption. Amit just did a better job of functioning in society.

She'd had a life once. She'd even had a boyfriend. Her nose stung and she swiped it with the back of her hand.

As if *that* was ever gonna work out.

After a few hours of companionable tapping, Amit pushed his chair away from the desk and reached both arms up to the ceiling that was crisscrossed with pipes. "I'm calling it a night. You sure you don't want to hit that party with me and Kelly?"

"I'm on a trail, so close." She grabbed the bottle of water she'd pulled out of her backpack earlier and chugged some. "But say hi to Kelly for me."

"Yeah, yeah. She's gonna give me hell for leaving you here by yourself."

Jerrica choked on her next sip of water. "She doesn't know we're Dreadworm, does she?"

"Who do you think I am?" Amit yanked a flash drive out of the computer. "You?"

"That's not fair." She wound her hair around her hand and tossed it over her shoulder. "I didn't tell anyone anything. He figured it out."

"Yeah, the last person who needs to know about Dreadworm—someone in the military."

Jerrica's cheeks blazed and she pressed the water bottle against her face. "Maybe that's why he was able to figure it out. He was Special Forces...*is* Special Forces."

Amit crammed some personal items into his bag. "And he never told anyone?"

"He wouldn't do that."

"Dude must've been crazy about you to keep that to himself."

"Crazy about me?" Jerrica snorted. "Yeah, so crazy about me he dumped me."

"Kinda hard for a guy in Delta Force to hang with someone who's trying to expose all the secrets of the federal government." Amit slipped his bag's strap across his body. "Dumping you is the least he could've done. It could've been a lot worse."

Jerrica pressed a hand over her heart and the dull ache centered there. "Don't you have a party to go to?"

"Outta here." Amit saluted and then tapped the monitor of the desktop computer. "Leave this running, please. I'm looking for some files connected to the attack on the embassy outpost in Nigeria. I know we didn't get the full story on that one, and I programmed a little worm that's chewing through some data right now."

She eyed the flickering display on Amit's computer. "See you later."

When the metal door downstairs slammed behind him, she shifted her gaze to the TV monitors to make sure nobody slipped into the building before the door closed.

Could she help it if paranoia sat beside her and whispered in her ear day and night? She'd been raised on conspiracy theories—and so far nothing in her life had belied that upbringing, nothing had stilled those dark undercurrents that bubbled beneath the surface of every encounter she had— even the most personal ones.

Amit disappeared from the security cam and Jerrica jumped from her chair and hunched over Amit's, folding her arms across the back and studying the data marching across the display.

The attack on the embassy outpost in Nigeria had been on her radar, too. And not only because it involved someone she knew, peripherally, anyway.

Delta Force Major Rex Denver had played a significant role in the Nigeria debacle, as he'd visited the outpost days before the attack. He'd also, allegedly, played a role in the bombing at the Syrian refugee center, although the witnesses in Syria had been walking back that narrative for a few months now.

She drummed her fingers against her chin. And Denver's name had come up again as she scurried down the rabbit hole of her current hunch—or maybe she'd been scurrying down a mole hole, if moles even burrowed into holes. Because she'd bet all the settlement money sitting in her bank account that the intel she'd been tracking was going to lead to a mole—possibly in the CIA itself.

Rubbing her hands together, she returned to her own chair and continued inputting data to dig deeper into the CIA system she'd already compromised.

After a few hours of work, she rubbed her eyes and took a swig of water. As she watched her screen, a blurry message popped up in the lower-left corner of her display.

She blinked and the words came into focus. She read them aloud to the room where all sounds of human intercourse had been replaced by the whirs and clicks of computer interaction. "Who are you?"

She huffed out a breath and growled. "You show me yours first, buddy."

So, someone at the other end had detected an intruder. She entered her reply, whispering the words as she typed them.

Who are you?

Not terribly clever, but she had no intention of showing her hand. She fastened her gaze on the blinking cursor, waiting for the response.

Her eyeballs dried up watching that cursor, so she set the program's command to keep running in her absence, just as Amit had done on his computer. If Amit came back to the Dreadworm offices, he would know to leave the program running, but just in case, she plastered a sticky note to her screen before packing up for the night.

Jerrica scanned the video feed showing the alley while she scooped up her backpack and hitched it over one shoulder. She swept up her black fedora, which she'd left here the other night, and clapped it on her head.

Flipping up the collar of her black leather jacket, she jogged down the steps from the work area. She tipped her head back to check the video from outside and then, pausing at the door, she pressed her ear against the cold metal, not that she could hear anything through it.

She took a final glance at the monitor above the door before easing the door open. She looked both ways up and down the alley. She shimmied through the space, the zipper and metal studs on her jacket scraping against the doorjamb, and pulled the heavy slab of metal shut behind her.

This alley had just a few doorways and a couple of fire escapes, so it didn't attract much traffic. Olaf, Dreadworm's founder, had searched high and low in Manhattan to find just the right locations, and then had secured those locations—but he hadn't been able to secure himself.

Someone outed him and his residence and he'd had to go on the run or face federal prosecution. She didn't want to be criminally charged, but she couldn't give up this job…mission…especially now that she'd hacked into the CIA databases.

She emerged from the alley onto the crowded sidewalk and joined the surge of people. Darkness hadn't descended yet on this cool spring evening. Summer with its heat and humidity waited right around the corner, and Jerrica wanted to soak up the last bits of May with its hint of freshness still on the cusp of the air. She closed her eyes and inhaled, getting a lungful of exhaust fumes and some guy's over-ambitious aftershave.

She headed underground to catch the subway to her neighborhood. Just as she plopped down in her seat, an old man with a cane scraping beside him shuffled onto the train.

Jerrica's gaze swept the other passengers in the car, their heads buried in their phones, earbuds shoved in their ears, noses dipped into tablets, reading devices and portable game consoles. Nobody budged, nobody stirred from the online, electronic worlds sucking up their attention and their humanity.

Jerrica hoisted her backpack from her lap and pushed up from her seat. She tapped the old man's arm and pointed to the empty spot.

He nodded and smiled, the light reaching his faded blue eyes.

The train lurched around a bend, and Jerrica grabbed the bar above her head, swaying with the motion of the car. Maybe she should've accepted Amit's invitation to the party. She didn't even have her cat to greet her at home. Puck had disappeared last month without a trace just as seamlessly as he'd entered her realm. Even cats had a way of passing through her life, perhaps recognizing her rootless existence and most likely identifying with it.

With both of her hands holding on for dear life, she shook her hair from her face. Yeah, she definitely needed to get out and socialize. She'd call Amit once she got home and had some dinner and put on her best party face.

The train rumbled into her station and she jumped off. She emerged into the fresh air but hung back at the top of the steps.

If someone had been following her this afternoon, they must've picked up her trail around here—her neighborhood, her subway stop. No way someone just started tracking her in the middle of Manhattan. She took a different route to Dreadworm every time she went there. This place, this neighborhood, comprised her only constants.

She zeroed in on a few faces, attuned to sudden stops, starts and reversals. She moved forward by putting one foot in front of the other because she had to start somewhere. Sometimes the fear and uncertainty paralyzed her.

She ducked into her favorite noodle shop and ordered a spicy vegetarian pho with tofu, inhaling the aroma of the rich broth while she waited for her order.

Kevin, the shop's owner, placed the bag in her hands. "Special for Jerrica. You find your cat yet?"

"No, I'm afraid he's gone for good, Kevin."

"I look out for him." He tapped his cheekbone beneath his eye with the tip of his finger. "Cats come and go."

So did people.

"If you do see Puck, give him some chicken and call me." She waved as she shoved through the door, sending the little bell into a frenzy.

She loped to her apartment, her pack bouncing against her back and the plastic bag containing the soup swinging from her fingertips. She could've afforded fancier digs, but this neighborhood on the Lower East Side suited her—and she'd found a secure building without a nosy doorman watching her comings and goings.

She made it up to her apartment, got through the triple locks and shut the door behind her. Her gaze flicked about the room, and a shot of adrenaline lanced her system.

She dropped her dinner, plunged her hand into the front pocket of her backpack and pulled out her .22.

"Get out here with your hands up or I swear to God I'll shoot you through the bathroom wall."

The door to the bathroom inched open and a pair of hands poked through the opening, fingers wiggling. "Don't shoot. I even brought a bottle of wine."

Jerrica lowered her weapon with unsteady hands and closed her eyes as she braced one hand against the wall.

Just like that, Gray Prescott had slipped past her best defenses…like he always did.

Chapter Two

Heavy breathing came at him from the other room, but he ducked his head anyway. He never could tell about Jerrica West. The woman didn't play by any rules.

Leaning back, he stuck one leg out the door. If she started shooting, he'd rather she take out a kneecap than his eyeball. "It's me, Gray... Gray Prescott."

For all he knew Jerrica could've wiped him from that databank she called a brain. When he'd ended their relationship over her hacking, she hadn't even blinked an eye as she showed him the door.

"I'm unarmed, and I need to talk to you, Jerrica."

A clunk resounded down the hallway. "C'mon out. I won't shoot...yet."

He poked his head out the bathroom door and whistled through his teeth. "I guess that was stupid to be in the bathroom when you came home, but I was washing my hands. I didn't know what time to expect you since I remembered you work late."

As he rambled on, he approached Jerrica as if stalking a wildcat. Her green eyes narrowed as he got closer, her heavy, black boots planted on the floor in a shooter's stance. He'd taught her that.

"What are you doing here and how the hell did you get in?" Her gaze flicked to the window that he'd left open a crack after climbing through.

"Yeah, well, I did come through that window, but the security for this building is good—better than most." He'd added that last part because he knew how important safety was for her, and he didn't want Jerrica freaking out right now.

"We're on the third floor." She pushed her black hair out of her eyes. "Oh, that's right, you're a hotshot Delta Force soldier able to leap tall buildings in a single bound."

"There was a fire escape, a ledge…and…forget it. I'm here now."

"What are you doing here? You said you wanted to talk—about what?" She crossed her arms over her chest not looking like she wanted to talk at all.

"Can we sit down and get comfortable? I wasn't kidding about the bottle of wine, and it took a lot of effort to get it up here. I left it in the kitchen." He pointed to the sofa with colorful pillows strewn across it. "You first."

"Where are my manners? I guess they went *out* the window, when you came *in* the window. It's not every day someone breaks into my apartment."

"It's not like I'm a stranger. I've even been to this inner sanctum before."

"Have a seat, and I'll get us a glass of wine." She finally uprooted her feet from the floor, and her heavy boots clomped across the hardwood to the kitchen. She grabbed the bottle of wine by its neck and raised it in the air. "How did you manage to break in here while carrying this bottle of wine?"

He wiggled his eyebrows up and down. "You have your secrets and I have mine."

"You don't have any secrets Gray. Nobody does." She jabbed a corkscrew into the cork, twisted and eased it from the bottle. The glasses clinked together as she pulled them out of the cupboard. "You use a computer? The internet? Social media? Buy online? Nothing is sacred. They know all about you."

"I know. You've told me before." He kicked his feet up onto her coffee table. "And after that cheery reminder, I'm gonna need a glass of wine more than ever."

She marched back into the living room, cupping a glass of wine in each hand. The ruby-red liquid sloshed with her jerky steps. She held a wine glass out to him. "You always did prefer red, didn't you?"

His gaze locked onto her lips, the color of the wine in her glass. "Yeah, I always did like red better."

Her cheeks flushed, matching her lips. She backed away from him and plopped down in the chair across from the sofa, pulling a pillow into her lap with one hand. "Now, what's so important that you need to scale a three-story building and break into my place, all while carrying a killer bottle of pinot noir?"

"I need your help, Jerrica." Damn, this was going to be harder than he'd expected. He'd better ease into it. "The kind of help only you can give me."

She swirled her wine in the glass before taking a sip. Raising her eyes to the ceiling, she swished the liquid around in her mouth as if at a wine tasting. "That's…interesting. What kind of help would that be?"

Gray gulped back a mouthful of wine. She was just trying to make this harder on him. Could he blame her? With a little more liquid courage warming his belly, he said, "You know. That hacking thing you do."

Her eyebrows disappeared into her bangs.

"What was that? Hacking? You told me that was illegal, immoral and un-American."

He snorted and the wine he'd just downed came up his nose. "I never said immoral."

"Whatever." She flicked her short, unpolished nails in the air, and the tattoo of the bird between her thumb and forefinger took flight—she also had one on her wrist. "The words and the accusations were coming so hot and heavy I couldn't keep track of them."

That hadn't been the only thing hot and heavy between them. He did his best to keep his gaze pinned to her eyes. If they wandered below her chin, he could expect one of those boots planted against his leg.

He spread his hands. "Give me a break, Jerrica. When we first started dating, I thought you were a generic computer programmer. Then you dropped the bombshell that you worked for one of the most notorious hackers out there, Dreadworm."

"I didn't drop any bombshell. You went snooping through my stuff." She rolled her eyes. "You really believed I was using you to get military secrets to post on Dreadworm?"

"Can you blame me?" He jumped up from the sofa and his wine came dangerously close to spilling over the rim. "If you had discovered I'd been lying to you, you would have gone underground and cut off all communications. Your reaction to my suspicion was laughable coming from one of the most paranoid people I know."

She bent forward at the waist and undid the laces on her right boot, hiding her face and buying time. He knew her well.

She pulled off the boot and got to work on the second one. She looked up, her bangs tangled in her long dark lashes. "You know now I never would've done that to you. You should've known it then."

He stopped his pacing to walk toward her, resting a hand on her shoulder, his fingers tangling in her silky hair. He rubbed a lock between his thumb and forefinger. "I knew it then, too, Jerrica. You just took me by surprise."

She shifted her head away from his touch and the diamond in the side of her nose glinted in the light. "Even if you weren't Delta Force, even if you didn't believe that I was using you, you're not a big fan of hacking, are you?"

"It seems…wrong." He stepped away from her and went back to his seat. "These are private government systems you're hacking. In some cases, these are classified systems. Communications not meant for the general public."

"All government systems should be for the general public." She tossed back her hair and raised her chin.

Gray took up the challenge. "Not if that exposure is going to result in outing people, putting their lives in danger, compromising their safety."

"Dreadworm never did that, and if you'd stuck around long enough to let me explain you would've known that."

"Maybe you're right. I admit I jumped the gun." He stretched his legs out in front of him. Now he had to get to the rest of his request. He tossed off the last of his wine.

"Looks like you need another." Jerrica pointed at his empty glass. "Maybe that'll help you get to the point."

"That obvious huh?" He pushed to his feet and held his hand out for her glass. "You, too?"

"I think I may need a few more to hear your request." She scrambled out of the chair and shoved her glass into his hand. "I brought some pho home for my dinner. Do you wanna share it with me? When I dropped the bag, the container even landed upright."

"Yeah, breaking and entering always makes me hungry." He took the wine glasses into the kitchen and filled them halfway. As he turned he almost plowed right into Jerrica. He lifted the glasses over her head. "Whoa."

The bag of food swung from her fingertips. "You're too big for this kitchen."

He surveyed the small space. "A jockey would

be too big for this kitchen. I thought you were going to move to a bigger place, a safer neighborhood. It's not like you can't afford it."

"I like this place. I feel secure here."

"I was able to break in." He set her wine glass on the counter at her elbow.

Nudging him with her hip she said, "You just told me my place was safer than most and it was your mad Delta Force skills that allowed you to break in here."

"I said safer than *most*, but you have the money to get into a much better neighborhood than this one with a doorman, twenty-four-hour security, the works. I don't know why you don't make the move." She picked up her glass and he clinked his against hers.

"You know I don't like using that money. Blood money." She took a quick sip of wine.

"You must use the money for living expenses, anyway. I can't imagine Dreadworm pays you the kind of salary to live in a Manhattan apartment without roommates. Didn't you tell me once that most of the other hackers have day jobs?"

"And didn't you tell me you came to Manhattan to ask me a favor?" She ladled the pho into two bowls.

As the savory steam rose, his eyes watered and he blinked, his nose already running from the spices. "Did I say it was a favor?"

"If it weren't a favor, Prescott, we wouldn't be standing around drinking wine and eating pho together. You're a man who likes to get to the point. You've been doing a lot of waffling." She slid a bowl closer to him and the tofu bobbed in the liquid like square life preservers.

He stirred the broth, chockful of health, with a spoon. "Figures you got tofu in here."

"Waffler." She puckered her lips and slurped up a spoonful.

This time, he allowed his gaze to linger on her mouth. If she wanted to see waffling, he could show her waffling by kissing her.

She wiped her nose with a paper towel, covering the bottom half of her face. "What's going on with you? What do you want me to do?"

He dropped his spoon in the broth and took a deep breath. "It's my commander, Major Rex Denver. He's in trouble."

"What kind of trouble?"

"He's AWOL, but that's not the worst of his problems."

"If going AWOL isn't the worst, it must be bad."

"He went AWOL because someone's trying to set him up."

Jerrica flinched and her eye twitched.

He hadn't even thought that Jerrica's own experience might make her more apt to help him, but here they were. She'd probably accuse him of using her again.

"I know."

His head jerked up. "You know about Major Denver?"

"Syrian refugee camp? Weapons stash at an embassy outpost in Nigeria? Fake emails?"

"Dreadworm really does know it all." He hunched forward on his forearms, pushing the bowl of soup aside. "That's why I'm asking for your help, Jerrica. You already know this info because you guys have access to all kinds of computer systems. We think there's someone on the inside manipulating data, emails, people to set up Denver and discredit him."

"Discredit him? Why?"

"Because he was onto something. Our Delta Force team was always operating one level beyond our special ops assignments. Denver was hot on the trail of some terrorist activity and someone was afraid he knew too much...or was on the verge of knowing too much." He reached out and grabbed her hand. "You understand more than anyone the government doesn't always operate on the up-and-up."

She withdrew her hand from his and sucked her bottom lip between her teeth.

Had he gone too far? He held his breath.

Her cell phone buzzed on the counter where she'd plugged it in to charge.

"Hold that thought." She raised her index finger.

Hold the thought? His appeal had gotten a better reception than he'd thought it would. He let out a noisy breath and picked up his pho again as she answered the phone.

"What is it? Thought you were at a party."

He almost spit out the pho he'd just put in his mouth. Did she have a boyfriend now? Just because he hadn't been able to move on after their breakup didn't mean *she* hadn't found someone to keep her warm at night.

"Wait, wait. Slow down. Who's following you? Did you get a look at him?"

This time he almost choked on some noodles. Listening in on Jerrica's phone conversations was proving hazardous to his health.

"Where are you now? Is Kelly with you?" She snapped her fingers at him and pointed to a pen and an envelope on the counter.

Maybe *not* a boyfriend. He shoved the pen and paper toward her and then went back to his soup, trying to concentrate on avoiding the slimy-looking veggies floating back and forth and to tune out Jerrica's escalating tone of voice.

"Stay right there. I'm serious. I'm coming." She glanced up at Gray. *"We're* coming."

He raised his eyebrows and tapped the handle of the spoon against his chest.

Jerrica nodded and ended the call, stuffing the envelope into her back pocket. "You wanted inside information on Denver? Here's your chance."

"What's this all about? Who was on the phone?"

"That was one of my coworkers at Dreadworm." She downed the rest of her wine. "He thinks he's being followed."

"What does that have to do with Denver?"

"Amit was working on delving into some classified correspondence regarding that weapons stash at the embassy outpost in Nigeria." She grabbed her backpack and slung it over one shoulder. "Denver was on that, wasn't he?"

"He was, and now your coworker is being followed." Gray cocked his head. "He's not…like you, is he?"

She wrinkled her nose. "What exactly does that mean?"

"You know, slightly paranoid."

She punched his shoulder with a right jab that made him flinch. "Get your stuff. We're meeting him in twenty minutes at a coffeehouse in the Village."

He grabbed his flannel and rubbed his shoulder. "Can we walk?"

"Subway. I'll make a New Yorker out of you yet."

As they raced down the building's stairs, Gray

poked her back. "Why are we running to meet Amit? If you need to talk to him in person, why doesn't he come here?"

"He's scared. I could hear it in his voice. That's the best time to get them talking."

"Dreadworm shares information with the world. Are you telling me that its employees don't share with each other?"

"Employees? We're not really employees."

She hiked up her pack and strode down the sidewalk of her Lower East Side neighborhood where people still milled around after their dinners and ducked in and out of shops. Gray kept pace with her.

Jerrica made a sharp right turn to head down the stairs to a subway station.

He followed her down and grabbed her arm as she started to push through the turnstile. "I need a Metrocard."

"Oh, I forgot." She led him to a machine and he purchased a single ride.

If Jerrica planned to dart around the city dragging him along with her, he'd better get a pass next time. But really, the woman had enough money stashed away to hire a car service. He did, too, but he felt about as disconnected from his money as she did from hers—probably for similar reasons. Neither one of them had earned the money on their own.

The subway swallowed them up and spit them out somewhere on the edge of Greenwich Village.

"Do you know where you're going? You haven't looked at the address since you wrote it down in your kitchen." He lengthened his stride to match her smaller but more numerous steps.

She patted the back pocket of her jeans. "It's right here if you wanna have a look, but I memorized it."

His gaze darted to her backside, shapely in her tight jeans, and his knees weakened for a second before he stuffed his hand in his own pocket. "That's okay. I trust that brain of yours."

"It's not much farther. Probably just around the next corner."

He didn't even bother asking her how she knew that. He'd accepted her calculating mind. What he couldn't accept was her guarded heart, but then he'd exceeded her distrustful expectations by dumping her once he'd found out she worked for Dreadworm. She'd fully gotten and relished the irony of his asking for her help, using the same skills he'd lambasted before.

He could live with eating crow—a lot of it—if it meant clearing Denver and getting to the bottom of this terrorist plot.

Jerrica tugged on his sleeve. "This way. You were about to pass it right by."

He veered to the right, dodging oncoming pedestrians. How could Amit know anyone was following him with all these people coming and going?

"This is it." Jerrica tipped her chin toward a building with a blue-and-white striped awning over the front door. "I hope he's still here and didn't get spooked."

Gray lunged past her to open the door, and the soft strains of a guitar melody curled around them, drawing them into a dark space where he caught a whiff of roasted coffee beans. He couldn't drink coffee at this time of night, but the smells took him back to late-night conversations with Jerrica, who seemed to run on the stuff when she was working on a gnarly hacking job for Dreadworm—when he'd believed she was just a programmer dedicated to her clients.

He glanced at her, eyes closed and nostrils flaring, getting a caffeine buzz off the fumes.

Her lids flew open and she scanned the room. "Damn, I don't see Amit."

"Do you want to get something and wait?" He gestured toward the counter. "I could go for a chocolate croissant."

"You go ahead." She swung her backpack around and dipped into the front zippered pouch, pulling out her phone. "I'm going to text him."

As Gray joined the line of mostly college students ordering complicated caffeinated concoctions, Jerrica hunched over her phone.

He reached the counter and ordered his croissant and a slice of lemon cake for Jerrica, even though she didn't know she wanted it yet. He dipped into his pocket for his wallet and twisted around. "Did he...?"

The strange woman behind him folded her arms and looked him up and down, a pair of pencil-thin eyebrows raised above her tortoiseshell glasses.

"Sorry. I thought you were my...friend. Did you see where she went? Black hair, about yea big?" He held his hand just beneath his chin.

She shook her head and went back to her phone.

"Sir, that's $6.75." The barista waited, a patient but trained smile on her face.

He handed her a crumpled ten. "Did you see where my friend went?"

"I didn't notice." She lifted her shoulders. "Maybe the restroom? They're around the corner."

"Thanks." Gray stepped out of line and waved his hand at the change on the counter, his heart beating an uncomfortable rhythm in his chest that didn't at all complement the strains of the folk music from the small stage.

He took the corner to the bathrooms at such high speed, he nearly plowed into a woman on crutches.

"I'm sorry." He pointed to one of the restrooms. "Anyone in there?"

The woman readjusted her crutch under her arm. "It's all yours. Good thing since you're in such a big hurry."

Gray maneuvered past her and tried the other door. "Jerrica?"

A gruff male voice answered him. "Nope."

Gray poked his head into the other restroom and confirmed what the woman on crutches had told him—empty.

He peered down the short hallway at a back door with a glowing Exit sign above it. Could Jerrica have gone out there to meet Amit?

He strode down the short, dark length of the hallway and pushed against the metal bar. He stepped into the alley, and held his breath against the odor of garbage coming from the overflowing dumpster to his left.

As he huffed the smell from his nose, a scraping, shuffling noise from beyond the dumpster made him cock his head. Adrenaline pumped through his body with a whoosh that left him light-headed…but just for a second.

His body shifted into gear and he launched past the dumpster.

Jerrica's face appeared to him as a white oval in the darkness for a split second before the lump crouching at her feet took human form, rose and slammed her body against the wall.

Chapter Three

The man drove his shoulder into her ribs as he smashed against her, pushing the air from her lungs. Her attention had been distracted by the appearance of Gray in the alley, but she couldn't wait for him to come to the rescue.

Her gaze shifted to the glint of steel on the ground. At least she'd knocked the knife from his hand when she bashed her fist against his nose.

She sucked in some air, coiled her thigh muscles and kneed her attacker between the legs. She didn't get as high or as much power as she'd wanted, but her lips twisted into a smile when he grunted.

The grunt turned into a wheeze when Gray materialized behind him and physically and forcibly removed him from her sphere.

Her assailant's body seemed to fly through the air, and his eyes bugged out of his skull. He yelled an expletive when he landed with a sickening thud, but he had enough strength or determination to extend his fingers toward his knife.

"Gray! The knife!" She panted as she slid down the wall into a crouch, all the strength seeping from her body.

Gray whipped around and stomped on the man's wrist with his boot.

The guy let out a howl that echoed down the alleyway and some shouting answered from the street on one end.

Gray scooped up the knife and turned his back to the broken man writhing on the ground. He kneeled in front of her. "Are you hurt? Do you need an ambulance?"

"No. No police or ambulance." She clutched at Gray's shirt with both hands. "He's getting away. Don't let him get away. He has Amit."

He cupped her sore face with one hand. "I'm not leaving you in this alley by yourself. He might have an accomplice."

She struggled to stand as her attacker staggered to his feet and limped off at a surprising clip, holding his arm.

"Is there a problem? What's going on?" Two men peered over Gray's shoulder, and he slipped the switchblade into his pocket.

"That guy was assaulting this woman." Gray jerked his thumb over his shoulder, but her attacker had already made it out of the alley and had turned the corner. "Now get lost."

The men immediately drew back in unison and muttered to each other as they took a hike.

Gray helped her to her feet. "Are you sure you're okay? I can take you to the emergency room and you can tell them you had a fall. You're good at covering up."

She hopped up on one foot, hanging onto his shirt. "I'm not okay. You just let the guy who was following Amit and attacked me escape. He has Amit and we let him walk away."

"He was limping away and how do you know he has Amit?" He rubbed her arms, brushing the dirt from her jacket.

"He texted me from Amit's phone. How do you think I wound up out here?" She gestured with her arm and winced.

"What I'm wondering is why the hell you scurried out to a dark alley based on a text without telling me." He ran his fingers through the hair hanging over her shoulder. "Dirt."

"I did tell you I was going outside. I guess you didn't hear me because you were so focused on ordering your chocolate croissant." She started toward the street, pressing one hand against her midsection.

"Where are you going and where are you injured?"

She leveled a finger at the street, teeming with traffic just beyond the alley. "I'm gonna look for the guy who bruised my ribs."

"You're not going to find him now, Jerrica." He patted the pocket of his shirt. "But I have his fingerprints. He wasn't wearing gloves."

She stopped and leaned against Gray's shoulder. "You're right. I'm not going to find him out there."

His arm came around her, and she put more pressure against his body, soaking in his warmth and power.

He squeezed her and his voice roughened as he said, "He had that knife. How'd you get out of it? When I got here, you had the upper hand."

"My senses were already on high alert. When I saw him out here instead of Amit, I knew something was wrong, so when he came at me I was ready. All those years of martial arts paid off. I gave him a quick shot to the face, and it startled him into dropping the knife."

Gray kissed the side of her head. "Ever think of trying out for Delta Force?"

She closed her eyes for a few seconds just to inhale the scent of him, all that clean masculinity making her feel soft and protected—even though she'd just kicked some guy's ass—almost. Feeling soft and protected was a dangerous place to be. The last time she felt soft and protected, her whole world had blown up.

She stepped back and shook her head. "They'd never have me."

"Let's go back inside. There's a slice of lemon loaf in there with your name on it."

He tugged on her arm and she went willingly, even though she couldn't stop looking over her shoulder.

She asked, "What do you think he did with Amit and why?"

Gray opened the back door of the coffeehouse and ushered her inside, the smell of coffee replacing the stench of garbage and fear that permeated the alley.

"I don't know. What did he want with you? Did he say anything? Was he trying to get you to go with him or was he trying to…kill you?"

"I'm not sure." She flipped her hair over one shoulder. "I didn't stop to ask him."

Gray seated her at a table, and keeping one eye on her, he retrieved two plates from the counter. He slipped the piece of lemon cake in front of her. "Eat."

She sawed off a corner. "This all has something to do with Amit looking into that arms stash in Nigeria. I'm sure of it."

"Which means it probably has to do with Major Denver. But why come after you?"

"Maybe because Amit called me, so they had my number. Maybe Amit didn't give them anything, and they thought they'd try me. They'd want to stop whatever hacking Amit is doing into that system."

"Stop how?"

"Get into Dreadworm's space and shut it all down. If the government is behind this, they've been wanting to shut down Dreadworm for years." She popped the bite of cake into her mouth and the taste of the sweet, tart lemon on her tongue almost erased the ashes left there by the conversation.

Had Amit divulged Dreadworm's location? If so, she'd have to mobilize Olaf's army to back up all the programs and data and physically move the computers before they were destroyed.

"Why don't you call Amit again—just for fun. Let's see what happens."

Jerrica caught a crumb of lemon cake from the corner of her mouth with her tongue and pulled out her phone. She scrolled to her recent calls and tapped Amit's name. Her stomach churned as she listened to the ringing on the other end. "No voice mail coming up. They must've turned off his phone. Do you think…?"

"No." Gray dabbed a flake of chocolate from his plate and sucked it off his finger. "They can't get anything out of a dead man."

"They can make him stop what he's doing. If they know he hacked into this classified system, Amit's death ensures that stops immediately."

"But it doesn't, does it?" Gray planted his elbows on the table on either side of his half-eaten croissant. "If he wrote a program to get into this secret database, that's going to keep running whether or not Amit is there to monitor it. Am I wrong?"

"You surprise me, Gray Prescott." She hunched forward and rubbed her thumb across a chocolate smudge on his chin. "You really *were* listening to me."

"I always listened to what you had to say, Jerrica. You're one of the most fascinating people I know. Why wouldn't I?" He placed the tip of his finger against his chin where she'd just cleaned it off.

"Because you hated everything I did, everything it implied."

"Hate?" He rubbed his knuckles against his jaw. "That's a strong word. I didn't believe what you were doing was right…or necessary."

"And now?" She folded her hands, prim as a schoolgirl, waiting for her absolution.

"I'm still not sure it's right, but it sure as hell is necessary. If people within the government are actively working against the interests of the US, those people need to be outed and stopped. Dreadworm can do that."

"It's worse than that, Gray, and you know it. These moles in our government aren't just working against us, they're working with terrorists to kill our fellow citizens. It's happening. We have all the pieces. Major Denver has all the pieces. We just need to fit them together to discover the who, what and when." She swiped a napkin across her mouth and crumpled it in her fist. "And we need to save Amit."

"Amit's going to have to save himself. Does Dreadworm have some sort of protocol in place that tells you what to do if one of you is…captured like this?"

"For communicating, but nothing for an abduction." She tossed the mangled napkin onto her plate. "You know Olaf went into hiding when he felt the snare tightening."

"It was worldwide news. Of course, I know." He reached across the table and entwined his fingers with hers. "When I heard that, all I could think of was you and your safety, and now here I am contributing to the danger."

Her heart fluttered when Gray said things like that to her, but pretty words didn't mean much. She hadn't been able to count on him before. He'd bolted once and he might do so again when he got what he wanted from her. It might be even worse this time if he felt guilty over his complicity in hacking into secure systems, but this time those systems belonged to rogue government employees, not the good guys as Gray had assumed.

Just because his family was so plugged into government service didn't mean all those nameless, faceless bureaucrats roaming the halls of Washington had the best interests of this country as their number one priority...or as any priority.

She disentangled her fingers from his. "You're not endangering me. I was onto this conspiracy before you arrived in New York, although I have to admit the data I stumbled on piqued my curiosity even more when I realized the person at the center of this swirling controversy was none other than your commander, Major Denver."

Gray cocked his head to the side. "You surprise me, Jerrica West."

"Why?" She slid her hands from the table and tucked them between her bouncing knees. Had she revealed how crazy attracted she still was to him?

"You remembered my Delta Force commander's name. I guess you *were* listening to me." He brushed his fingers together over his plate, a smug little smile playing about his lips.

Listening? She'd hung on to every word out of his mouth, never quite believing he was truly hers or would stick around. And she'd been right.

"You had some interesting stories, yourself."

"I thought..." He shrugged his broad shoulders, and a tide of color rushed into his face.

She narrowed her eyes. "You thought what?"

"Once I learned about your line of work, I thought your interest in me had more to do with what I could reveal about our defense than me personally." He thumped his fist against his chest.

"You said something like that before and it's idiotic." She grabbed her purse and shot up from her chair. "Let's go."

He followed her toward the door so closely she could feel his warm breath stirring her hair. For a good-looking guy, Gray had a surprising number of insecurities. His well-connected family had mega bucks, and she'd figured it always had him wondering if women wanted him or his family's wealth and connections.

With her own stash of cash in the bank from the settlement and the modest way she lived, he'd never been able to accuse her of going for the gold, so he'd made up another reason that she'd be interested in him.

She tossed her head and flicked her gaze at the many women tracking his progress out of the cof-feehouse. Did the man have a mirror?

When they hit the sidewalk, she took his arm. "I'm worried about Amit. We have to find him before they hurt him."

"Or break him."

"That's not going to happen." She pulled him toward the subway station. "Olaf's army is loyal. We don't break."

"You may not break under the gentle, monitored, *legal* questioning of the government, but that's not what we're dealing with here. If these are government agents, they're not your mother's government agents."

She tripped to a stop at the top of the stairs leading to the platform. "*Your* mother's, maybe. They're exactly my mother's and my father's."

As she trotted downstairs, tears blurred her eyes and Gray put a steadying hand on her back.

He ducked his head to hers. "Sorry. Stupid thing to say."

When they boarded the train, she gripped the pole and swayed toward him as the car moved forward, her eyes locking onto his dark blue ones.

She shuffled closer to Gray, almost whispering in his ear. "Amit's in danger, isn't he?"

"You're *both* in danger."

"I have to tell Olaf. Maybe we should go to the Dreadworm offices now." She chewed on her bottom lip, all the sweetness of the lemon cake gone.

"And get followed? Not a good idea." He pinched her chin between his thumb and forefinger. "Stop doing that. You'll make it bleed."

"You're right. Now is not the time to go running off to Dreadworm. That's what they'd expect." She slid a gaze to the side. "Someone could be on our tail now."

The train squealed as it rolled into their stop

and the force threw her against Gray's chest. She rested there for a few seconds, long enough for Gray to balance his chin on top of her head.

"We'll figure this out. We'll find Amit."

As she pulled away from him, strands of her hair clung to the scruff on his jaw, connecting them for seconds longer, seconds she needed to collect herself.

They hustled down the sidewalk, shoulders bumping, and she'd never felt so safe—except for the last time Gray had been with her in New York—before he found out what she did.

When they reached her building, one of the other residents pushed through the door and held it open for them, nodding at Jerrica. She gave him a hard stare.

The door closed behind them and Gray watched her curiously. "You don't know him?"

"I do, but he's never seen you before in his life. How'd he know you were with me?"

Gray raised his hand clasping hers. "Maybe this is a hint."

"You never know. I could be your captive." She studied Gray's face, but he didn't even roll one eye. That attack had scared him as much as it had her.

They clumped up the stairs, their boots filling the staircase with noise. Jerrica placed her hand against her door and turned the first lock.

She froze as icy fingers played up her spine. Then she hissed between her teeth. "Someone's been here."

Chapter Four

Gray's muscles tensed and he stepped between Jerrica and the door. He bent his head to hers, his lips brushing her ear. "How do you know?"

"This lock." She circled a piece of tarnished metal with her fingertip. "It locks from the outside with a key. I locked it when we left, and now it's not locked. The other two lock automatically when the door closes."

"Unlock the rest and stand back." He hovered over her shoulder as she shoved her key into two more locks, clicking them open.

Earlier, he'd taken one look at that line of locks on Jerrica's door and figured he'd have better luck coming through the window. Had someone else come to the same conclusion and then left through the front door?

Or was that someone else still waiting inside?

As he pushed into the room, he clutched the gun in his pocket and tensed his muscles. A breeze ruffled the curtains at the window—the same window he used earlier.

"You didn't leave a window open a slice, did you?"

"Absolutely not."

"Stay back." Nobody had jumped out at them or appeared with guns blazing, but that didn't seem to be their style. The guy in the alley had had an opportunity to stab Jerrica when she first went out there, but he'd wanted something else.

He pulled the gun from his pocket and followed it into the room, raking his gaze from side to side. Jerrica's possessions, in place and undisturbed, belied the presence of an intruder.

Tipping back his head, he scanned the loft. From his vantage point, nobody had disturbed Jerrica's neat space. If it weren't for that lock and the window open a crack, they'd have no reason to believe anyone had compromised her apartment.

Together, they walked into the guest bedroom downstairs and Gray checked the closet and the bathroom.

Jerrica gasped and his finger tightened on the trigger.

"My laptop's upstairs."

Lunging after her, he reached out to grab her but she twisted away from him and stomped up the rest of the stairs. He had no choice but to follow her, his panic causing him to pant.

As Jerrica dove for the laptop on the nightstand, Gray threw open the closet doors. The mostly dark-colored clothes shimmied on their hangers. His hands plowed through the materials, skimming leather and denim and soft cotton, but no intruders crouched in the recesses of the closet.

He took a step back and bumped into the foot of Jerrica's bed where she was sitting cross-legged, hunched over her computer.

"They didn't take your laptop? That's weird." His eyes darted around the neat, bare room, as impersonal as a jail cell, and he took a deep breath. "Are you sure someone broke in?"

She raised her gaze from the laptop and her green eyes narrowed. "I knew right away. I always secure that lock. They underestimated me if they thought I wouldn't notice that, the window...or other things."

"Such as?" Again, his gaze wandered around the spare room.

"I can't explain it to you—it's the placement of a book, the angle of a cushion. They didn't want to leave a mess. Didn't want me to think they'd been here." She dug her fingers into her black hair, and pulled it back from her face with one hand. "That's why they left my laptop."

"If they didn't take anything and didn't want to scare you by tossing your place, then what?"

She flicked her fingers at the computer. "They're going to track me through this."

Gray's heart jumped. "How would they do that? *Can* they do that?"

"Keystrokes."

"You lost me, just like you always do with this stuff." He sank to the bed and an unexpected flash of desire scorched his flesh as he remembered the last time they'd been on this bed, in this room.

Jerrica gave no sign that the memory had crept into her databank. She ducked her head, her straight hair creating a curtain around her face as her fingers flew across the keys.

"The intruders probably loaded a program on my laptop that's going to send anything I do straight to them—anything I look up, any emails, any programs I run. That's what I'd do. It'll be like they're looking over my shoulder while I work."

"You think you can find it?"

She peeked at him through the strands of her hair and snorted, causing the black curtain to flutter about her face. "No problem."

As Jerrica sank farther into the zone, Gray slid from the bed and jerked his thumb over his shoulder. "I'm going to head downstairs and see about securing that window so nobody, including me, can get into your place that way again."

Jerrica murmured without looking up.

He'd been in this situation with her before and knew better than to disturb her.

Jogging downstairs, he skimmed his hand along the bannister and jumped off the last step. He curled his fingers under the window and shoved it open the rest of the way. He leaned out, looking down into the street from the third-floor drop.

The tree abutting the building offered wily climbers, like him, access to the ledge running along the side of the apartment building. He couldn't get rid of the tree, but he could do something about the ledge and the window itself.

He pivoted away from the window and into the kitchen. He threw open a few cupboard doors until he found a bottle of olive oil. Too bad Jerrica didn't have cooking spray, but he didn't expect to find anything that unnatural in her kitchen.

He unscrewed the lid of the bottle as he walked back to the window and then drizzled the contents along the ledge below. A slick surface wouldn't allow someone the grip he needed to hang onto the side of the building. He set the empty bottle on the counter and tipped back his head, calling up to the loft.

"Do you have a hammer and some nails?" He had to yell twice before Jerrica emerged from her fog.

"What?"

"Hammer and nails? Where do you keep your tools…if you have any?"

"Toolbox on the floor of the front closet. Why? Never mind. Carry on."

Crouching before the closet, he clawed through the coats and scarves hanging to the floor and wrapped his fingers around the handle of a metal toolbox. He dragged it out and flipped open the lid.

Jerrica kept the toolbox as neat as everything else in her life—every nut and bolt had its place. He messed them up before selecting several long nails and a hammer, wrapping his fingers around the black rubber encasing the handle.

He returned to the window and nailed it shut. As he tapped the final nail into place, Jerrica appeared behind him, her hands on her slim hips.

He met her gaze in the window's reflection.

"You just nailed my window shut."

"That's right. Nobody can get through it."

She reached over his arm and traced a nailhead with her fingertip. "Someone could smash it."

"And crawl through jagged glass? I don't think so." He turned to face her and they stood chest to chest, neither of them moving or pulling away. "Besides, I poured oil on the ledge. Nobody is going to be able to hang on it or stand outside the window long enough to be able to break it or cut it."

Her eyes widened and he got the full effect of those green orbs. "You poured oil on the outside of my building? What is this, 1066 and you're defending the castle?"

"It wasn't *hot* oil. It's an effective method—as long as it doesn't rain several days in a row." He pulled on his earlobe. "Your building manager isn't going to suddenly power wash the building, is he?"

"Did you actually get a look at my building while you were scaling it? I don't think it's been washed in a hundred years. Wait. What kind of oil?" She spun around, her black hair lashing his cheek.

He rested his hand on her shoulder as he pointed to the bottle on the counter. "Olive oil."

"Are you securing my building or making hummus?"

"Hummus?" He sniffed. "Why would I make hummus? It's the only oil I could get my hands on. If you were a normal person, you'd have some cooking spray on hand. That would've been a lot easier to use."

She wrinkled her nose. "Cooking spray has chemicals you don't want anywhere near your food."

"I'm sure it does." He raised his hands. "Don't ruin cooking spray for me like you ruined red meat."

"Does that mean you gave it up?" Turning her head, she raised one hopeful eyebrow.

"Not quite. I just try not to think about you while I'm ripping into a juicy steak." He snapped his mouth shut and sealed his lips. Had he just admitted to her that he thought about her? A lot?

She shifted away from him and reached for the empty bottle. "I guess I'll have to put olive oil on my grocery list."

He cleared his throat. "Did you get done what you needed to get done up there? Did you find the bug or the program or whatever?"

"I did not. Nothing was loaded on my computer." She sucked in her bottom lip. "Maybe they weren't smart enough to do something like that."

Gray methodically surveyed the small, neat space—not a cushion was out of place. "What did they do here, then?"

Shrugging, Jerrica splayed her hands in front of her. "I don't know. I would think they'd want to hit my laptop. They want to know what we know—or what we're going to discover. But they couldn't break into it and didn't want to take it and alert me."

A knot formed in the pit of Gray's stomach as his eyes darted around the room. Maybe the intruder didn't take anything. Maybe he left something behind.

"Gray." Jerrica grabbed his arm. "What are we going to do about Amit?"

His gaze shifted to Jerrica's face, her forehead creased and her mouth turned down. His fingers itched to smooth the lines from her face, to turn up her lips. "Unless you want to call the police, there's not much we can do right now. Do you have his girlfriend's number?"

Her frown deepened. "No. I wish she would call *me*. Maybe we could get some info out of her. Maybe she saw someone or something."

"Would she call the police if she doesn't hear from Amit?"

"I'm not sure. He lives…"

Gray put two fingers against her lips and shook his head.

Her eyes got round but her mouth tightened with understanding. She grabbed his hand. "It's late and I'm tired. I'm going to soak in the tub for a bit before I go to bed. Do you want to join me?"

Even though he knew it to be a ruse, his heart thumped at the thought of sharing a tub with Jerrica. "Lead the way."

She headed for the stairs and he followed her, his gaze dropping to her derriere outlined in a pair of tight black jeans. Jerrica didn't follow the latest fashions, but her urban guerilla style pushed all his buttons. This time his buttons would remain pushed…no release. The sexual tension coiled in his gut until he gave himself a mental shake when Jerrica pushed open the bathroom door.

Remember why you're here. What's at stake.

He slammed the door behind them, and Jerrica hunched over the tub and cranked on the faucets full blast.

"You think that's enough?" The running water almost drowned out her whisper.

"I think that'll do it." He lifted a framed photo of a woman in an old-time swimsuit from the wall, ran his hand along the back of it and around the edges of the frame.

As Jerrica twisted her fingers in front of her, he lifted the lid on the toilet tank and scanned the dry parts. Then he pointed to the mirrored medicine cabinet.

Jerrica swung open the door and studied the inside as if deciding which medicine to take. "I don't see anything. You?"

"No, but we're not talking freely outside of this room until I do a search with my cell phone."

"Your cell phone?"

He plunged his hand into his pocket, pulled out his phone and tapped the display. "I have a program on my phone that will detect audio devices."

"That's handy. How come I don't know about

that?" She tipped her head back and her gaze darted to the four corners of the ceiling. "Cameras?"

"I doubt it, but I'm going to check for those, too. I'm pretty sure whoever is tracking you is more interested in what you say than what you do."

"And who I do it with?" She pointed a finger at him.

"Me?" He swiped a hand across the back of his neck as the steam from the hot water swirled around him.

"If these people are aware that Denver's Delta Force team members are the only ones actively working on his behalf, you can bet they know who you all are at this point."

"You're probably right." He reached forward and plucked a strand of hair from Jerrica's moist face. "Yours is exactly the kind of mind needed for this situation."

She cocked her head. "Only for this situation?"

"Hell, I'd be happy to have you by my side in *any* situation, Jerrica West." He ran his thumb along her lower lip. "I'm trying to remember if we said anything revealing out there before it dawned on me that they might have bugged the place."

"As far as I can recall, we spent most of our time talking about olive oil."

He snapped his fingers. "At least they'll know they can't get into your place again."

"We talked about Amit, but they know more about him than we do." She sank to the edge of the tub. "What have they done with him? If they have his phone, they must have him…or worse."

"They're not going to kill someone if they want to get intel from him." He slammed a fist against his chest. "Take it from someone who knows."

"I don't want to hear about what you do." She made a cross with her fingers and held it in front of her face. "But if Amit refused to give them what they wanted, refused to take them to Dreadworm, they'd have no more reason to keep him alive."

"They would if they thought they could change his mind." He sat down on the tub next to her and draped his arm around her shoulders as the water rose behind them. "I know it's hard, but try not to think about Amit right now. When that guy had you cornered in the alley, he could've killed you with the knife, but he didn't."

"I should warn everyone else, send out messages. Olaf has a warning system in place and neither Amit nor I used it. We just panicked."

"That's understandable." He squeezed the back of her neck, and then glanced over his shoulder. "I think we'd better turn off the water before it overflows, but until I do my search of the rest of the house, no talking about anything related to Amit or Olaf or Dreadworm."

"Or Major Denver." She reached around him to turn the faucet, her soft breast momentarily pressing against his arm.

Closing his eyes, he swallowed. "You're not going to waste all that water, are you? You stay here and relax while I do my thing."

"I'm not going to miss this search. I can help." She flicked some water at his chest. "The tub can wait."

Gray left the bathroom first, tapping the display on his phone to bring up the program that could detect radio waves. He headed into Jerrica's bedroom first and waved the phone over her headboard and the framed pictures on the wall above it.

Jerrica joined him and pointed to the closet.

He shook his head. Any sound would be muffled before it reached a mic in the closet. He continued to move around her room, wielding the phone in front of him as if warding off evil spirits.

As he passed the phone in front of the second nightstand, he heard a clicking sound. He brought the phone close to his face and watched the line on the display flicker.

Jerrica tugged on his sleeve and he nodded as he crouched before the nightstand. He felt around the base of a lamp and inside the shade, his fingers stumbling across a disc stuck to the inside.

He picked it off with his fingernail and cupped it in the palm of his hand to show Jerrica. She aimed a rude gesture at the little bug, and he grinned before he strode into her bathroom and dropped it into the toilet. He flushed it down and brushed his hands together.

As Jerrica started to open her mouth, he covered it lightly with his hand and pointed at the floor. Downstairs, he found the same type of listening devices attached to a lampshade next to the sofa and on the underside of a cupboard.

Jerrica sighed as he disposed of the last bug. "Do you think that's it?"

"I hope so. These wouldn't be hidden inside cupboards or closets because that would reduce their efficiency. I'll keep the program up and running on my phone, just in case, and I'll give the spare room and bathroom a once-over before I go to bed."

She whipped her head around. "You're sleeping here tonight?"

"I sure as hell am not leaving you here on your own after everything that happened today, and if there are any more bugs, they'd hear me leave. That's not happening."

"What hotel are you staying at?" She stood at the sink and rinsed out their dishes from earlier this evening, which now seemed days ago. "Wait. Let me guess."

He grabbed her fingers in the stream of water. "Yeah, it's a nice place. And don't act like you couldn't afford to stay there with me, but tonight I'm staying with you."

"Touché." She wriggled her hand free from his and flicked some droplets of water at *his* face this time. "The bed in the second bedroom is made up. Towels in the bathroom closet, unless…"

She pushed away from the counter and grabbed a dish towel from the oven door handle. "Yeah, I'm not gonna let that warm water go to waste. I need to wash the grit from that alley off my body, anyway."

"Toothbrush?" He tipped his head toward the hallway, reluctant to leave the small enclosure of the kitchen where he felt like he could keep Jerrica close to him.

"There should be some extras in that bathroom closet."

"Try to relax." He nudged Jerrica out of the kitchen and walked with her to the stairs, afraid to let her out of his sight.

She turned at the top of the stairs and held up her hand in a wave. "Thanks."

When she disappeared into the bathroom and clicked the door shut, he rested his head against the wall for a few seconds, almost feeling the warmth course through his body as if he were slipping into the embrace of the water with Jerrica between his legs.

He tapped his jaw with his knuckles. This wasn't the right time to rekindle a relationship with Jerrica…even if she wanted it.

Gray turned the corner into the hallway and entered the second bedroom, waving his phone in front of him. The intruders hadn't bothered bugging this room or the bathroom. He dropped to the made-up bed, kicked off his shoes and peeled off his shirt.

He'd brush his teeth and hit the sack. The only shower he needed right now was a cold one—and he'd rather wallow in his X-rated thoughts about Jerrica for a while longer.

A half hour later, Gray crawled between the sheets, running his tongue along his minty teeth, and pulled the covers up to his chin. When he'd gotten the message from Denver about contacting Jerrica West to ask for Dreadworm's help, he hadn't hesitated for a second. How much of that was due to his desire to clear his commander's name and how much was his desire to see Jerrica again, he didn't know and he didn't want to analyze. He'd call it a draw.

A muffled buzzing noise interrupted his hazy thoughts and he bolted upright in the bed. He cocked his head, and as the sound continued, he threw back the covers, grabbed his weapon from the nightstand and bounded across the room.

He stumbled into the hallway, and Jerrica called from the bathroom upstairs.

"It's the door to the building. Don't let anyone in."

As if he needed her to tell him that. He crept toward the computer display Jerrica had set up in her entryway, his gun dangling at his side, and swiped the mouse.

Hurried footsteps padded down the stairs and Gray looked over his shoulder to take in Jerrica flying down the steps, a white towel wrapped around her slim frame.

He turned back to the display and the image of the street, and the front of the building appeared on the screen…along with a tall figure bent over at the waist, his face hidden.

Gray mumbled. "C'mon buddy. Show yourself."

As Jerrica joined him, her hand resting on his shoulder, the man at the door dropped his head back and peered at the camera, his swollen face distorted and bloodied.

Jerrica dug her fingers into Gray's flesh. "Oh my God. It's Amit."

Chapter Five

Adrenaline pumped through Jerrica's body, and she reached over Gray's shoulder for the release button to unlock the door.

Before she got midway there, Gray snatched her hand. "Wait."

"Wait for what?" She clutched at the slipping towel with her other hand. "Can't you see him? He's been beaten. He needs our help."

"We don't know what they've done to him, Jerrica. It might be a trick. They probably followed him." Gray's jaw hardened and she recognized the look.

She dug her heels into the floor as her fist curled around the terry cloth under her arms, holding the towel in place. "What does it matter? They already know where I live. They've been inside, planted bugs."

"They might've armed him with something. Maybe he's wearing a wire."

She twisted her fingers in his grasp, which he

tightened. "They already tried that, and we disrupted their plan. We'll do it again, even if Amit is wired. He's not going to turn on me, anyway."

"You don't know that. You don't know what they're capable of doing to make people bend to their will." A muscle twitched at the corner of Gray's mouth, and the tension radiated off his body.

"I know my…friend's in the street, battered and bloody, and he came to me for help—and you always called *me* the cold one." Maybe she'd never considered Amit a friend before, but they were in this together now. She released the hold on her towel and slammed her thumb against the button to unlock the front door. She leaned toward the speaker. "Come up, Amit…and hurry."

When she'd let go of the towel, it had fallen to her feet, and goosebumps raced across her naked body.

"Stubborn woman." Gray swept her towel from the floor and bunched it against her midsection. "Stay here. The guy can't even make it up the first flight of stairs by himself."

She shook out the towel and twisted it around her body, securing a corner. "A-are you going to help him?"

"Yeah." He leveled a finger at her, nearly touching it to her nose. "Watch the display and make sure nobody slips in behind him or tries to ambush us on our way up."

She nodded as Gray gripped his weapon in front of him and lunged past her to the front door, his boxers hanging on his hips. He slammed the door behind him.

Jerrica's nose stung as she watched Amit sag against the door. He'd been capable of just enough steps to get him inside the building, but he hadn't moved since.

Her heart slammed against her chest as a dark figure moved into view. When she realized it was Gray, she gulped in some air to steady her breathing.

Amit had Gray by a few inches in height, but Gray had the muscle and he used it to good effect as he hitched Amit's arm around his shoulders and wrapped his own arm around Amit's body. He half-dragged, half-carried Amit toward the stairs.

Jerrica's eyes burned as she watched the display for any unusual movement behind them or further attempts to breach the front door. When she heard their thumping and bumbling footsteps in the hallway, she peeled her gaze away from the monitor and clawed at the locks on her door.

She swung it wide and gasped as Gray dragged an unconscious Amit into her apartment. "What happened? Why did he pass out? Is he still alive?"

"He's alive. He lost some blood." He settled Amit onto the floor. "Get some towels—wet and dry. Ice. Whiskey."

Jerrica scurried to the closet in the downstairs bathroom and snatched several hand towels from the shelf. She filled her arms with some first aid supplies and dumped everything next to Gray, crouching beside Amit. Then she bunched one of the towels in her hand and made for the kitchen where she left it under the faucet as she filled a plastic bag with ice and grabbed a bottle of tequila from the cupboard above the fridge.

She dropped to the floor next to Gray, his fingers resting against Amit's pulse, and dabbed his facial wounds with the damp towel. As she wiped away the blood, she blew out a breath.

"It looks worse than it is."

"Stanch the blood flow from the back of his head. That's the deepest cut, the one that's bleeding the most." Gray raised Amit's eyelids with his thumb. "We could take him to the emergency room."

"No." Jerrica pressed a dry towel against the wound on Amit's head and unbuttoned his shirt with trembling fingers. "That would bring cops and questions. Dreadworm has strict protocol about that. Amit knows."

"If he doesn't respond soon, we have no choice.

I'm not going to sit here and watch someone die. What's Dreadworm's protocol on that?"

She ran her hands across Amit's chest and around his back. "No wires. He's not hooked up."

Gray raised an eyebrow. "Any wounds on his body?"

"None of those, either." Heat suffused her cheeks. "You're the one who warned me about wires."

"Relax. I know." He traced some red spots splotched across Amit's chest and abdomen. "Looks like he took a beating to the midsection."

"At least they used fists instead of knives." She replaced the cloth at the back of Amit's head.

"Check his pockets, too." Gray picked up the bottle of booze. "Tequila?"

"I don't drink whiskey. That tequila is the closest thing I have. If you want to clean his wounds, I have antiseptic for that." She shoved one of her hands in the front pocket of Amit's jeans.

"I wanted to try to give him a sip to see if it revives him. Tequila might work." He unscrewed the lid from the bottle and tipped it toward Amit's lips. The clear liquid ran down the side of his face to his neck. "Guess not."

Jerrica dumped the coins she'd dug out of Amit's pocket onto the floor and searched the other one. She held up a scrap of paper. "Just an old receipt."

"Check his back pockets for a wallet." Gray hoisted Amit into a sitting position, placing his back against the foot of the couch. "I'm going to try to wake him up."

Reaching beneath his body, Jerrica patted Amit's back pockets. "Nothing."

"Amit! Wake up." Gray took Amit's jaw between his thumb and forefinger and squeezed as he shook his head back and forth. "Wake up."

"More tequila?" Jerrica doused the corner of a towel with the alcohol and squeezed a few drops into his mouth while Gray pinched it open.

Amit's dark lashes fluttered, and Jerrica patted him on the cheek. "Amit! It's Jerrica."

He groaned and turned his head to the side to escape Gray's fierce grip.

"Lighten up." She circled her fingers around Gray's wrist. "He's bruised enough."

"I want him conscious." Gray grabbed the bag of ice and applied it to the side of Amit's head.

Amit's eyes flew open and he gasped, as if sucking in air after a near drowning. His eyeballs rolled back in his head for a second and then he focused on her face. "Jerrica?"

"Thank God." She grabbed one of his thin hands and chafed it between her own, even though he wasn't cold in the least. "What do you need?"

Amit sucked in a breath and squeezed his eyes closed. "Everything hurts. Where am I?"

"You're at my place." She exchanged a quick look with Gray. "Do you remember coming here?"

"Yeah." His hazy gaze wandered to Gray. "Who…?"

"He's a friend. He's going to help us. Can you tell me what happened tonight? When we got to the coffeehouse, you were gone."

Amit's head dropped back against the sofa, as he clutched his middle.

"Let's help him onto the bed." Gray rose to his haunches and curled an arm beneath Amit. "Can you get up?"

Amit staggered to his feet with Gray's help, and walked on wobbly legs to the bedroom. "Kelly. I have to call Kelly."

"We'll make sure she knows you're okay." Jerrica squeezed past the two men into the spare bedroom where the covers were still turned down after Gray's quick exit from the bed. She bunched the pillows against the headboard and patted the mattress. "Put him here."

Gray eased Amit's broken body to the bed and propped him up. "Try to stay alert for a while. We'll get you cleaned up and tend to your wounds. Do you need to go to the hospital?"

"No!" Amit winced with the effort of his yell. "No hospitals. No police."

"Then you'd better not die on us." Gray turned from the bed and left the room.

Jerrica unbuttoned the rest of Amit's shirt and peeled it from his shoulders. "Can you tell me what happened?"

"Like I told you on the phone, I was being followed. I sent Kelly home with friends because I didn't want either of us to be followed to our place. I ducked into the coffeehouse because I thought I'd be safe in a crowd." He closed his eyes. "I was wrong."

"Did they strong-arm you out of the coffeehouse?" Gray had returned to the bedroom, carrying the first aid supplies.

Amit opened one eye and assessed Gray. "Is he…?"

"He's safe."

"I meant, is he the Navy SEAL?"

Gray cleared his throat. "Delta Force. What happened in the coffeehouse?"

"Ouch." Amit jerked his head back as Jerrica pressed the ice pack against his temple. "Some guy followed me in there with a knife."

"I wonder if he's the same guy who attacked you in the alley, Jerrica. He must've figured you'd come after Amit at the coffeehouse." Gray sat on the edge of the bed and shook a bottle of ibuprofen in the air. "Take a few of these. You'll need them for those ribs."

Amit's eyes widened as much as they could. "Someone attacked you, too?"

"We went out to the coffee place, and I received a text from you. I went out to the alley to meet you and was met by a guy with a knife instead."

"They took my phone." Amit popped the pills and chased them down with a slug of tequila. "You actually went into the alley to meet someone? You?"

"That's what I said." Gray flicked a strand of Jerrica's hair.

"Not the smartest move, but I guess I was desperate to find you, Amit." She brushed her hand across her cheek and the growing warmth there.

"Don't worry. I didn't tell them anything. I didn't lead them to Dreadworm."

Jerrica folded her arms over her stomach. She probably deserved that. Of course, Amit would think she'd be more worried about Dreadworm than his safety. He'd be wrong. She'd learned a thing or two after Gray dumped her. Had learned she could hurt people as much as they'd hurt her. She hadn't liked the realization.

Gray lifted one eyebrow. "How'd you get away from them? Did they let you go in exchange for leading them to more Dreadworm hackers? Leading them to Jerrica?"

"Hey, no." Amit made a grab for the bloody towel against the back of his head as it slipped to his shoulder. "They didn't let me go. A cop saved me."

"You went to the police? You just said no police." Jerrica pursed her lips.

Tapping his bruised forehead, Amit said, "You're not thinking very clearly, Jerrica, which is a first for you. After the guy roughed me up in the alley, he started marching me at knifepoint out to the street to what I guessed was a waiting car and more torture in my future. Luckily, there was a group of unruly drunks on the sidewalk that had caught the attention of two cops. I broke away from my captor a few feet in front of the cop and fell onto the sidewalk. The guy with the knife disappeared into the crowd, taking my wallet and cell with him."

"What did you tell the officer?" Jerrica placed a hand against her chest, trying to tame her galloping heart.

"Told him I'd had an altercation of a personal nature in the alley and didn't want to make a report or press charges." Amit raised one shoulder. "He was only too happy to let it go. I would never lead them here, Jerrica."

"They made it here, anyway." She swept a hand

through the air. "In fact, they may be listening to everything we've been saying."

"They broke into your place?" Amit's gaze darted around the room. "What do you mean, listening to us?"

Gray pushed off the foot of the bed and took a turn around the room. "When we got back here, Jerrica insisted someone had broken in. Nothing was missing and she couldn't detect any activity on her computer, though. They wouldn't break in and leave with nothing, so I swept the place for listening devices. We found several and dispatched them. We were just turning in until…"

"Until I showed up and ruined the party." Amit glanced at Jerrica and his gaze dropped to the towel still wrapped around her body. "Aren't you cold?"

"Freezing." She rubbed her bare arms.

As if noticing his own state of undress for the first time, Gray yanked his shirt off the top of the dresser and pulled it on. "Go upstairs and put on some pajamas. I'll finish dressing Amit's wounds."

As Jerrica backed out of the room, she said, "Don't get to any of the good stuff without me."

Upstairs in the loft, Jerrica let the towel fall to her feet. She slipped into a pair of pajama bottoms and a matching top, pulling it over her head with her hands still trembling.

Both she and Amit had been attacked in one night, but their attackers hadn't gotten what they wanted…not yet. She had a feeling they wouldn't stop until they did.

She jogged downstairs and walked in on Gray and Amit talking about the attack. "What's the verdict? Is he gonna live?"

"He took a beating, but he'll be okay." Gray stuffed the last of the bloody towels in a plastic garbage bag. "Some bruised ribs, a few cuts, and he'll have a black eye for sure."

"Why did he pass out?"

"In case you haven't noticed I'm not a doctor, but I'm guessing blood loss and exhaustion. He did try to keep his abductors away from your place, so he was wandering around for a while and riding the subway."

Amit touched the bandage on the back of his head. "For not being a doctor, you did a good job."

"I've had some practice patching wounds." Gray dropped the bag by the door. "Now, let's figure out what these people want."

Jerrica sat cross-legged on the foot of the bed. "The keepers of that shadow government database must've figured out that Dreadworm had compromised it."

"But how do they know who we are? I'm a mild-mannered computer programmer by day.

Kelly doesn't even know what I do at night." Amit waved his hand at Jerrica. "You're an independent on-call computer nerd. How are they following us and breaking into our homes?"

Gray asked, "Who are the other Dreadworm people who work here?"

Amit held up two bony fingers. "Cedar and Kiera. I mean, there are others in other locations, but we're the only four in the New York area and only Jerrica and I are in that particular office. Nobody else knows about that location—except Olaf. We don't see much of Cedar or Kiera. If they have a location like we do, we don't know where it is. Olaf tends to keep us separate."

Jerrica said, "We need to send out an SOS to them. We've definitely been compromised. They could be in danger, too."

"Unless they're the ones who outed you." Gray rubbed his chin. "Think about it. They did it or Olaf did it."

"Wait." Jerrica held up her hands. "Those are only the people we know of who know our identities. There could be others—*you* know I work for Dreadworm and you apparently told Major Denver because *he* knew. Who else knows? Where else is it circulating?"

"Guilty, but I know Denver didn't ID you, and I sure as hell didn't."

"Did you tell your other Delta Force team

members? You know how that goes. They tell someone innocent and they tell someone innocent, and eventually the intel gets to someone who's not so innocent."

Gray shot her a look of annoyance from beneath a set of scowling eyebrows. "Let's start with the inner circle first."

"For whatever it's worth, the guy who was beating me up didn't ask any specifics about Dreadworm. He warned me to stop meddling. Told me what we were doing was only helping the government."

Jerrica sliced a hand through the air. "Dreadworm has never been about bringing down the government. It's about making it better, more accountable to the people."

"This guy seemed to think that would be a persuasive argument for me." Amit stifled a yawn. "Did one of those happy pills contain codeine or something?"

"You needed it for the pain." Gray nudged Jerrica in the back. "And now we all need some sleep. We can continue to untangle this in the morning."

Amit shoved a pillow beneath his head. "Is it safe here? You said someone broke in."

"Don't worry. I'll handle the security."

"Kelly." Amit's lids drifted closed. "I need to tell Kelly."

"Keep Kelly ignorant and safe for now, Amit. We'll find some way to get word to her, and I'll send out an alert to the others." Jerrica shut off the light and pulled the door shut.

Kicked out of his bed, Gray veered toward the living room and the smallish sofa.

Jerrica grabbed his hand. "Don't be an idiot. You can share my bed upstairs. I don't bite… anymore."

Gray chuckled, but a look of panic flashed across his face. Did the thought of being in bed with her make him think twice about his motive for being here?

"I don't mind the sofa. I've slept on worse."

"I'm sure you have, tough guy." She placed her hands against his back and gave him a little shove up the stairs. "But you're back in civilization now."

His back and shoulders held military stiff, Gray trod up the stairs as if meeting a firing squad. Maybe she should've let him sleep on the couch.

In the loft, she flicked on the lamp where they'd found the bug and turned down the covers. "I did finally invest in a king-size bed, so there's plenty of room for both of us."

She slipped under the covers and turned off the light.

As he crawled into the bed as far away from her as he could possibly get without falling out, she cleared her throat. "I'm glad you showed up today, Gray. Both Amit and me would've been lost without you."

Rolling onto this back, he pulled the covers up to his chin like a virgin on his wedding night and growled. "Like I said, I'll take care of the security and you can do your hacking thing. We need to uncover this plot and exonerate Denver. At this point, I think you're the only one who can do that."

"Nice of you to think so, anyway."

"Good night, Jerrica."

"Good night, Gray."

She slid a sideways glance at his profile in the darkness, noticing his wide-open eyes staring at the ceiling, his hands at his sides. Maybe he was just keeping alert for safety.

She had to know one way or the other. She wanted him. Needed the comfort of his body.

"Gray?" She stroked his corded forearm with her fingertips, and it was as if she'd brought a statue to life.

Chapter Six

Gray's body shuddered and shifted as he answered her, his voice hoarse and gruff. "Yeah?"

A million words rushed through her brain, formed and discarded. This didn't have to be perfect. It just had to be honest and true. She said the words that had been running through her brain all day.

"I want you."

Gray seemed to burst from the tight cocoon he'd been inhabiting and rolled to his side, reaching for her.

She went willingly into his arms, her head fitting in the crook of his neck as if it belonged there. It did.

He stroked her hair back from her face. "Are you sure?"

"Are you? You're the one who walked out on me." She pressed her lips against the tight skin over his collarbone.

"Dumbest thing I ever did." He skimmed one

finger down her spine. "I thought you were using me to get information. It bruised my ego, and I couldn't get over that."

She snorted. "You don't have an ego, Gray. As if any woman wouldn't want to be with you for you—I never cared about your money, your political connections or the military intel you could provide—I knew you'd never go down that road, and I never would've asked you. I thought *I* was the paranoid one."

"I should've known. I *did* know that." He cupped her face with his hand and kissed her hard on the mouth.

She murmured against his lips. "Can we stop talking now?"

He answered with his touch, flattening one palm against her belly and circling up to her breast in a slow, sensuous movement that had her squirming. When he reached her nipple, he traced it with one fingertip. After one gentle pinch, he undid the top few buttons of her pajama top. He then grabbed the hem and pulled the top over her head.

She kissed the firm line of his jaw. "Keep doing what you were doing before, you tease."

"No one's ever accused me of being a tease before, including you." This time he placed both of his hands on her breasts, now aching for attention, and stroked and shaped them to his pleasure…and hers.

She tugged at his T-shirt. "Why are you wearing this?"

"I was trying to be prim and proper and put as much material between me and you as possible." He dragged the shirt from his chest, dispensing with prim and proper.

"Why? D-do you feel guilty for being here in my bed? Is it for the wrong reasons?"

"I'm not sure what the right and wrong reasons are anymore, are you? I just know I've never been able to stop thinking about you, but I didn't know how you'd feel about seeing me again."

"Excited, elated…and very, very turned on."

She pushed away from him to drink in the sight of the hard slabs of muscle shifting across his chest. She outlined the planes with the tips of her fingers, skimming through the dusting of dark hair sprinkled over his flesh.

Brushing her nails across his flat abs, she said, "Is this a twelve-pack now?"

"It's whatever you want it to be." He slipped his hand beneath her pajama bottoms and underwear and smoothed it over the curve of her derriere. "All this time, I've been aching for your touch, and I couldn't even muster the strength to tell you I was sorry for how things ended—for my part in it. I needed my commander to order me to contact you."

"Umm, I don't think I gave you much reason to believe I'd ever accept your apology or want to see you again."

He grabbed her hands as they inched their way down to the waistband of his boxers. "I'm thinking we should've had this talk before we hit the sheets together."

"It's not like we've had time to discuss our relationship." She hitched her thumbs in the elastic of her bottoms and yanked them off, along with her panties. "Besides, I can talk and play at the same time."

"Really?" He made a mocking face. "I dare you to try."

He cinched her around the waist and flipped her onto her back as he straddled her naked body. The kisses he rained on her face, throat, chest and belly had her gasping and arching her body for more.

As he flicked his tongue across her navel, she gritted her teeth and gasped out, "As soon as you accused me of using you for intel, I should've realized you were equating me with all those other women interested in your family's money and power."

Resting his chin on her abdomen, he glanced up at her. "That's quite a mouthful. I'm failing you."

He trailed his hands between her legs and nudged her thighs apart, his hot breath moist against her swollen flesh. "Care to continue your analysis of my insecurities?"

She opened her mouth, but he had moved so he could plunge his tongue inside her and the only thing coming from her throat was a squeak. She felt his smile hot against her skin.

Several words flitted across her brain, but the only one she could manage as his tongue prodded her was, "Oh."

Her fingers curled into his thick hair and her nails dug into his scalp as he brought her closer and closer to her release. For several moments, time stood still as she hung on a precipice of desire, her breath coming out in short puffs, every nerve ending alight with fire.

Gray scooped his hands beneath her bottom, tilting her toward his greedy mouth. As he pinched and kneaded her soft flesh, her passion reached dizzying heights. Her temples throbbed with the tension until she let out a tiny breath.

That small act of submission opened the floodgates, and her orgasm swelled inside her, infusing every pore in her body with sweet release.

Gray kept his mouth locked onto her, riding every wave as it crested and then crashed, teasing her back up again and again until her body opened to him completely.

Satiated and limp, she lacked the energy to even guide his erection into her as he prodded her with its insistent head.

After a few thrusts where he filled her completely and then slid out, she returned to some semblance of sense and reason. His performance deserved an active partner, and she wrapped her legs around his hips, holding him to her. She raised one arm to brace herself against the headboard as he rode her.

He hitched up to his elbows and stared into her face as if committing it to memory. All of her memories came flooding back with the heaviness of him between her legs. She sucked his bottom lip between her teeth, nibbling at the softness.

A drop of sweat rolled down Gray's face, and every part of his body seemed to get harder. His gaze rose to a point above her head, and she knew he was close. By the time they'd split up, she'd been able to read every nuance of his lovemaking. They'd been able to read each other, allowing them to fit together like two pieces of a puzzle.

Her other half released something between a growl and a moan as he plowed into her with quick, sure strokes. A flush rose from his chest and suffused his face as he reached the peak.

She watched the pleasure soften the features of his face, and she brushed her knuckles against the stubble on his chin. Tears pricked the back of her eyes as he lowered his body on top of hers, spent and satiated, the weight of it making her feel protected and secure.

She'd always scoffed at the notion of making love. Sex had been a function just like anything else in life, one partner easily swapped for another—until the day she met Gray Prescott.

He'd swept her off her feet in a way that belonged in movies and fairy tales—ones she'd never believed in before.

Although their backgrounds couldn't be more different—he from a wealthy, politically connected, privileged family, she from an outlaw commune, tracked and raided by the very government his family represented—Gray had felt their similarities almost immediately. He'd known her from the beginning, knew what she needed before she did.

That's why it had hurt so much when he turned from her. He should've known she'd never try to compromise him—not even for Dreadworm.

"Am I crushing you?" He shifted his damp body to the side and kissed her ear. "You can continue talking now, if you want—if you remember what you were saying."

Rolling toward him, she hitched her leg over his hip and curled her toes in feline satisfaction. "I don't even know if I remember how to talk after that. You leave me speechless."

"You leave me breathless." His heavy hand shaped the curve of her hip. "We weren't under the covers one minute before you made your move. Did I make it that obvious that I wanted back in your bed?"

"I wasn't sure at first. You came off as very professional, forced to see me again because Major Denver demanded it."

He took a lock of her hair and swept the end of it along his jaw. "It was a good cover. I'd been wanting to reconnect with you for a long time—as soon as I realized what an ass I'd been about the whole Dreadworm thing. Denver gave me the perfect opportunity, a chance to reconnect and to prove to you that I trusted you."

"How could you be sure you'd get the response you wanted from me?" She drilled a finger into his chest. "We left on bad terms, throwing accusations like flowerpots at each other."

"And hurting ten times more than flowerpots." He touched her nose with his fingertip. "Even if you didn't want anything to do with me personally, I knew you wouldn't have been able to pass up a chance to use your hacking skills to ferret out a conspiracy. It's your lifeblood."

"Is it?" She rubbed his muscular backside with her hand as he flexed it. "I'm beginning to think something else is my lifeblood because I've felt adrift without you. I mean, adrift was my middle name growing up, but you gave me something different. I missed it when you left. Craved it."

"I never knew any of that when we were together."

"Maybe I didn't, either." She turned her back to him and dragged one of his arms around her waist.

He nuzzled the back of her neck, and a thrill ran down her spine. Who knew the one thing that had driven Gray away would be the catalyst to bring him back into her life?

A pinprick of fear needled her brain. *Unless he's using you and Dreadworm to save Major Denver and plans to disappear just as completely as before.*

JERRICA WOKE UP to an empty bed, as usual, but this time it was unexpected. She swept her hand across the cool sheets beside her, just in case she'd missed the six-foot-tall, muscle-bound man who'd rocked her world last night.

The clinking from the kitchen downstairs brought her upright, and she sniffed the air. The rich smell of coffee swirled its way up to the loft and put a smile on her face. When she heard Amit's voice waft upstairs, her smile grew broader.

They'd just scaled one hurdle in this mess,

Amit's safe return, but it was a big one and she'd take it for now.

She dove under the covers to retrieve her discarded pajamas and underwear with a smile twisting her lips. If Gray had thought he could come into her bed and actually fall asleep, he must've forgotten how things were between them.

She hadn't.

Scrambling into her pajamas and hopping on one foot, she called downstairs. "Save some coffee for me."

When she reached the kitchen, Gray was hunching over the small counter that divided the kitchen from the living room, cupping a mug of coffee in his hands. Amit faced him, a bag of ice clutched to his eye.

"How are you feeling?" She poked Amit's arm on her way into the kitchen, and he winced. "Not so good?"

"I feel like a truck ran over me and then reversed to do it all over again." He put the ice down to curl his fingers around the handle of a steaming mug. "And we're trying to figure out how to reach Kelly to let her know I'm okay, without putting anyone in danger."

"I think we should contact the other two New York-based Dreadworm hackers. If you two have been compromised, maybe they have, as well." Gray held up the coffee pot. "You want some?"

"What do you think lured me down here?" Jerrica swung open a cupboard door and snatched a coffee cup from the shelf. As she held the cup out to Gray, she said, "We have procedures to contact Kiera and Cedar. We'll put those in place this morning. Kelly is another matter."

Amit patted the front pocket of his shirt. "If I had my phone I'd call one of her friends, but I don't have any of those numbers memorized."

"What about social media sites?" Jerrica dipped into the fridge and popped up holding a small carton of cream. "Can you get to her friends via social media? Post something or private message them?"

"I can do that." Amit traced the bandage on the back of his head. "Don't know why I didn't think of that before. I'm losing it."

Gray slurped at his coffee and eyed Jerrica over the edge of the cup. "What's the procedure for contacting Kiera and Cedar?"

"Message boards." She dumped some cream into her coffee and watched the white swirls invade the dark liquid. "We're supposed to check a couple of TV message boards daily for information or put an alert on our phones for message replies. That's how Olaf communicates with us, too. I'll put out the SOS that Amit and I have been made."

Amit tipped some cream into his own cup. "We have to check on the equipment."

"You could lead them right to Dreadworm if they're following you." Gray raised his eyebrows. "And it seems as if they are."

"I agree with Amit." Jerrica tapped her fingers on the counter. "We have to try. If those computers have been compromised, we have to shut down our operations."

"Can you do that remotely?" Gray asked.

Jerrica widened her eyes. "You mean do it anyway without checking? No way. We'd lose whatever inroads we've made into this stealth government database—the same database that's been keeping track of Denver's activities."

Gray dumped the rest of his coffee in the sink where it splashed up on the sides of the stainless steel. "We don't even know what these guys look like, which would help in spotting a tail. How are we going to know if they're following you?"

"We do know. We both saw him last night when he attacked me in the alley, and we've already determined he's the same guy who abducted Amit."

"That's one guy, and he could've been wearing a disguise." Gray held up his index finger. "Do you really think he's working on his own? Do you think he's the same one who broke in here? There could be dozens more."

"We'll wear our own disguises—God knows, I have a few. And we can get out of this building without going through the front door." Jerrica folded her arms and leaned against the counter. "We have to get to Dreadworm."

Amit shoved his coffee cup toward her. "And I have to contact Kelly. Can I use your laptop?"

"It's upstairs." Jerrica left the men in the kitchen and took the stairs two at a time up to her loft. She swept the laptop from the nightstand and tucked it under her arm as she jogged back downstairs.

When she hit the bottom step, she crooked her finger at Gray and Amit. "Join me on the couch."

Amit limped across the room with Gray by his side, his hand on his shoulder. Amit lowered himself stiffly to the sofa cushion beside her.

Biting her lip, she turned to him. "I don't think you should leave this apartment, Amit. Gray and I can go to Dreadworm."

Amit sucked in a breath as he pressed his fingers against his temple. "It's my work."

"I get it, but you're going to stand out and if we have to make a quick getaway, you're going to be in trouble."

"She's right." Gray dropped to the sofa on the other side of her. "Jerrica will be able to tell if the Dreadworm space and the work have been compromised."

"All right, all right." Amit collapsed against the

back of the sofa and closed his eyes. "Try Becca Landau. She's one of Kelly's best friends."

Jerrica shoved her computer onto Amit's lap. "You'll have to log in with your account. I have a fake one and if I try to private message Becca, she may never see it. If you two are already friends, she'll look at it."

Amit opened one eye. "I have a fake account, too, but Becca knows who I am. She'll recognize the name I use."

As he bent forward, Jerrica put a hand on his back. "They really did a number on you."

"No kidding." Amit logged in under his phony name and clicked on Becca Landau's profile. "This is it. What should I put in the message?"

"Just ask her to tell Kelly you're safe but can't reach out to her right now." She tapped Amit's arm as he began typing. "And tell her not to say anything to anyone else, and Kelly shouldn't, either."

Midway through the message, Amit's fingers froze. "What if they know where we live? They must if they followed us to the party. Is Kelly going to be safe? What if they grab her to get to me?"

"Can she leave town?" Jerrica tugged on Gray's sleeve. "Should she leave town, Gray?"

Gray chewed on the inside of his cheek and Jerrica's pulse jumped because she recognized the look. He was about to deliver news he didn't want to deliver.

"If she has someplace to stay, that might be best." Gray tipped his head toward the laptop. "Add that to the message."

Amit's Adam's apple dipped as he swallowed. "You're not kidding, are you?"

"I'm afraid not. This is not the US government. You've crossed people who have no rules. They are a law unto themselves, and they'll go to any lengths to achieve their results. We already know that and shouldn't take any chances."

Amit's fingers flew over the keyboard. When he finished his message to Kelly's friend, he eased back against the sofa. "I can't believe I dragged Kelly into this."

"It'll be okay, Amit." Jerrica patted his knee in an awkward attempt to soothe him. They'd really never been anything more than coworkers up to this point. She didn't kid herself that Amit had run to her for comfort. He'd come to her because he thought she could help…and that was okay.

Amit's gaze dropped to her hand, and she shifted it. "I'm not like you, Jerrica. You live and breathe this stuff—and I know why."

She snatched her hand away from his leg. "What does that mean?"

"Just because you're the best hacker at Dread-worm doesn't mean the rest of us aren't damned good. I've known about your background for over a year now."

"What do you know?" Jerrica laced her stiff fingers together.

Amit glanced at Gray, who shrugged.

Jerrica waved her hand at Gray. "He knows everything about me." *Almost everything.*

"I know that your father ran that compound down in New Mexico and that the government raided it, he fought back and both of your parents were killed."

Jerrica eased out a breath and loosened the tight grip of her fingers as Gray rubbed a circle on her back. "Good work. Yeah, that's my legacy, but it doesn't mean I want to continue living my life looking over my shoulder."

Amit snorted softly through his nostrils. "Okay. And I definitely don't want to live *my* life looking over my shoulder."

Gray swept the computer from Jerrica's lap and pushed up from the sofa. "Then you're in the wrong line of work, Amit. What you two are doing with Dreadworm invites scrutiny. I don't know what you expect. Olaf is in hiding."

"We don't expect to get killed." Jerrica jumped from the sofa. "Do you want Dreadworm's help or not to get the information about Major Denver?"

"You know I do, but I don't like seeing you in

danger—either of you." Gray wagged his finger between her and Amit, still slumped on the sofa.

"Like you said—" Jerrica turned toward the staircase "—we're in the wrong business."

An hour later, they had settled Amit back in bed with a gun beside his right hand, and Jerrica had sent out the SOS codes to their Dreadworm coworkers in the city.

As Jerrica slid the final lock on her apartment door into place, Gray asked, "Are you sure the doors to the utility room and alley are going to be unlocked?"

"I used this exit fairly recently." She jabbed him in the ribs. "You're as nervous as Amit."

"He's right, you know."

"About what?" She hoisted a small backpack over her shoulders and grabbed the bannister on her way down.

"You've always lived your life in a state of paranoia."

She shook her head. "Not you, too. Give it a rest. I didn't grow up behind the white picket fence like you did, with all the comforts and privileges, but I turned out halfway normal, didn't I?"

"Normal enough for a home and kids?"

Jerrica almost tripped and she clutched the bannister for support. "Are you asking?"

"Just wondering." He tugged on her backpack. "I'm not asking anything until I know the answers."

"That's a cowardly way to live your life." She broke away from him and jogged down to the first floor of her building, as much to hide her confusion as to make sure they could escape this way. Was Gray really thinking about marriage and children?

Could she get that close to him without revealing everything?

She tried the handle to the door that led to the basement utility room. "It's open."

Gray followed her down another flight of stairs, breathing heavily.

"Are you out of shape, D-boy?"

He sneezed. "It's dank down here."

"It's where we keep the trash." She pointed to another door past a row of dumpsters. "But it's where the building next door keeps its trash, too, so this is our ticket out."

"What's on the other side?" Gray strode past her and grabbed the handle of the metal door.

"Stairwell landing—in the other building."

As Gray yanked on the handle, Jerrica held her breath, but the door creaked open. Poking his head into the space, he said, "All clear, just as you said."

He held the door wide for her and she brushed past him, strolling into the other building.

"We don't even have to go to the first floor and out the front of this building. There's a door that leads to the side alley, so even if someone is watching the back of my building, we won't be going out that way."

"Perfect." Gray blew out a breath he'd probably been holding since they hit the stairwell. "You've developed the skills you needed for the job you do."

"You can thank Olaf for that."

Gray's eyes flickered in the semidarkness, and Jerrica sealed her lips. Gray had always felt a twinge of jealousy about her relationship with Olaf. The man had recruited her specifically for Dreadworm based on her past. Gray didn't know half of her complicated relationship with Olaf, but not one ounce of that relationship contained anything remotely akin to romance. But she had no intention of revealing any of it to Gray. It might lead to other revelations—ones she wasn't ready to expose.

"Maybe Olaf should've practiced a little of what he preached. He might be a free man right now."

"He's free."

"He's in hiding."

"He's still free."

"If you can call it that." Gray lifted one shoulder and then wedged it against the door. "Okay to open?"

"It's now or never."

"Wait." He pulled his weapon from his pocket and held it close to his body as he eased open the door.

The cool air from the alley flooded the stairwell, and Gray held up his hand. "Stand back for a second."

He stepped outside first and then cupped his hand and motioned her forward.

She joined him in the empty alley and tugged her hat down over her ears. "Quick getaway."

"You're a genius." Gray kissed the side of her head.

"On to Dreadworm."

By playing lookout and bodyguard, Gray made the path to the Dreadworm office easier than ever. They made so many twists and turns to get there, nothing less than a bloodhound could've tracked them.

When they reached the door on the alley, Gray peeked up from beneath the bill of his baseball cap. "Cameras?"

"Cameras, locks, sensors. The works."

They slipped into the building and Jerrica let the heavy door clang behind them. "It's upstairs."

"Nobody should be here, right?"

"That's right. Just Amit and I have access to this site. So, if anyone got to our stuff, they did it remotely."

"And you don't even know where the other Dreadworm site is in the city?"

"Nope. And they don't know the location of ours—not that we don't trust each other." As Jerrica climbed the stairs with Gray behind her, she swept off her cap and tousled her hair. She sighed when she reached the top step. "Everything looks good."

"But you can't tell until you look at the computers, right?"

She tipped her head. "You're learning." She dragged her chair out from her workstation and plopped into it.

Her fingers on the keys woke up the computer and she checked through her processes. "Still working and still making headway into the stealth database."

"Amit works over there?" Gray jerked his thumb toward another bank of computers.

"Yeah, and I have his codes. He didn't have a choice." She sat in Amit's chair and cranked it up so she was eye level with the displays.

"He's coming at the database from another angle, but it's the same database of communications and email traffic. I know he's looking at the weapons stash in Nigeria, but I'm not completely sure where he is with that. We don't necessarily share."

She entered Amit's passwords to access his

computer and tapped into the dark government database that they'd both stumbled onto.

With Gray hovering over her shoulder, she flicked her fingernail at the monitor as lines of text scrolled down the screen. "This is it. I think he broke in even further."

"What does it all mean? What are those lines of text?"

"They're entries in the database—emails, files, even text messages."

"And these are the people setting up Denver?" He dragged over a stool and straddled it. "Can't you just enter some search criteria to narrow down the conversations?"

"We can and we have, but most of the text is in code. Even if we search for Denver, for example, nothing will return because his name isn't used in the messages. We would have to crack the code first, and that's not necessarily what we do—even Olaf."

"Then it's a good thing others do it." Gray's hands shook as he scrabbled for the phone in his pocket.

Jerrica pressed a hand against her chest. "What are you saying? Do you have the code deciphered?"

"Some of it." Gray scrolled through his phone. "Try entering these words—fickle, Monday, scope."

Jerrica stopped the scan process and switched to a search mode. "Repeat those words."

Gray said the three words again, and Jerrica entered them into the search field. The words popped up on the screen in yellow highlight.

"Can you print this out?" Gray jabbed a finger at the screen.

"I will, but let's not wait." She swung the monitor toward Gray. "Can you do it online?"

"Yep." He tapped his phone and held it up to the screen, mumbling under his breath, his gaze tracking back and forth between the computer and the phone.

He swore and smacked his phone facedown on the desk. "This is it, Jerrica. This database is outlining the plan."

"What plan?"

"The plan to stage a sarin attack on US soil and blame it on Major Denver."

Chapter Seven

Gray could barely get the words out of his mouth, past his thick tongue. These people, whoever they were, planned to pin this on Denver. How? Why?

Jerrica blinked. "Sarin? This is the plan Denver was uncovering?"

"Who is this, Jerrica?" Gray slammed his fist next to the keyboard. "Who are these people?"

"Can't tell you that yet. All we know is that it's connected to the government, but it's not a standard government database. It's under the radar. There's not a name or a government official we can connect it to."

"We need to find out before this attack is carried out."

A crease formed between Jerrica's eyebrows. "How are they going to blame Denver for this when he's still missing?"

"That'll make it easier for them." He skimmed a hand across his head. "Denver's going to have to come in. If he's under military arrest, he can't be blamed for anything."

"Really?" Jerrica scooted back her chair and crossed her legs at the ankles. "He can still be accused of the setup if not the implementation."

"I wonder if Denver knows any of this?"

She flicked a finger at his phone. "He must, if he's the one who gave you the code."

"He did give me the code, which he got from someone else, but he doesn't have access to the files here." He hunched forward and planted his elbows on his knees. "Nobody but us has access to this. Do you think all this data is going to tell us who's behind the plan? It has to be someone high up."

Jerrica cinched his wrist. "Maybe you can help with that, Gray. You know these people. You rub elbows with them."

He searched her green eyes for the usual signs of disdain reflected there when she spoke of his family. They glinted back at him with hope and enthusiasm.

Her grip on him tightened. "Can you do it? Will you do it?"

"If it means getting to the bottom of this and stopping a terrorist attack, of course. I don't have any loyalty to people who are willing to destroy this country…do you?"

Jerrica's cheeks flushed and the jewel in her

nose glinted as she flared her nostrils. "I never did. That's not what my family was about."

"All right. I'm not going to get into a battle of the families here." He brushed a lock of black hair from her hot cheek. "But in case you haven't noticed, we're in New York and my family and my family connections are all in DC."

"Maybe we need to take a trip to DC to visit your family. They know you're stateside? I can't imagine you're here on official business."

"I'm not. I'm on leave, and my family knows it. They did invite me to their annual Memorial Day bash, though. That might be the place to start."

"Then it's time for a family visit."

He cocked his head at her. "You never wanted to meet my family before—when we were together."

"I didn't figure they'd be all that interested in meeting the daughter of Jimmy James. I thought you were keeping me away from them. Did you even tell them you were dating the daughter of the infamous survivalist who got into a shootout with the FBI?"

As Gray answered, he shifted his gaze to his phone and the code Denver had sent. "I told them."

"And?" Jerrica tapped the square toe of her boot on the cement floor.

"They weren't thrilled." Gray shrugged it off. His parents' opinions about the women he dated, even this woman, didn't matter to him.

Jerrica traced the edge of her phone. "Is that why you dumped me?"

"That had more to do with your work at Dreadworm…and your association with Olaf…than any outside opinions. And that was a mutual dumping."

"Only because you were acting like an ass." Her lips pressed into a tight smile. "And now here you are."

"Who's acting like an ass now?" He ruffled her hair. "Don't rub it in."

"I'm glad you're here." She dropped her long lashes and jerked in her chair. "Speaking of codes, I just got an alert from Kiera's message board. I need to check it."

Jerrica sprang up from the chair in front of Amit's computer and scurried to her own desk. As Gray looked over her shoulder, she brought up a website with a discussion board for a popular TV show.

"Zombies? That's appropriate." Gray drew up a chair beside her as she clicked on a message thread.

"What are you looking for?"

She ran her finger down the user names. "A message from Deadgirl."

Gray slapped at a prick of uneasiness on the back of his neck. "Laying it on kinda thick, isn't she?"

"It fits for the venue. Don't read anything into it." She hopped in her seat. "There she is."

Jerrica clicked on a message from Deadgirl and read aloud. "I think they should've blown up the bridge to Bristol to stop the zombies, and my favorite episode this season is five."

"Okay." Gray scratched his chin. "Do we need another cipher decoder to figure this out?"

"No, we have our own code. Bristol stands for Washington Square Park and episode five is the time, so she wants to meet at Washington Square Park at five o'clock. The zombies? You can figure that out. Easy."

"Maybe too easy?"

"Who would know to look for our communications on a discussion board for a TV show?"

"That gives us some time for lunch and to start deciphering the communications from this database. We know the what and where, but we still need the when and the who to stop this thing."

"I suppose the why doesn't matter, does it? The whys are always the same—power, control, probably money."

"You don't really believe what your father built had nothing to do with power and control, do you? He was an autocrat. He ruled that compound with an iron fist."

She whipped her head around. "I never defended what he did, but the FBI didn't have the right to come in and kill innocents."

"Jimmy James opened fire first, Jerrica. You told me the story yourself."

"I know, but the women, the children? My mother, my brother…" She put a hand over her eyes as the pain stabbed her heart.

Gray scooted closer and wrapped his arms around her. "I know. I'm sorry. Everyone knows it could've been handled differently. That's why your lawyers got you such a huge settlement."

"Blood money." She dashed a tear from her face, and then pointed at Amit's computer. "That has to be done printing out soon. When it is, we'll get lunch and bring something for Amit—along with the good news that we can decode the databases we found."

"Deal." He pinched her chin between his thumb and forefinger and kissed her forehead.

Jerrica didn't like talking about the raid on her father's compound, which he'd egotistically and ironically called Jamestown. Jimmy James had been stockpiling weapons and ranting and raving against the government for years, starting to challenge authorities on government lands. The

FBI had reacted and then overreacted, and Jerrica had lost her entire family in the shootout.

Lawyers had swooped in on behalf of her and the other survivors, and she'd won a multi-million-dollar settlement and had been sent to her mother's sister, eventually taking her aunt's married name, West.

Jerrica had a reason to be paranoid and he'd hated to further enforce that paranoia, but the world they inhabited was a scary place.

Olaf, who'd once worked for the federal government, had taken advantage of Jerrica's situation. He'd recruited her, groomed her to be a hacker and eventually take over Dreadworm. Gray didn't trust the man or like him.

"Earth to Gray." Jerrica snapped her fingers in his face. "The printer has finally stopped. I'll find a manila envelope and put that tome in my backpack."

"Yeah, okay." He pointed to Amit's computer. "Should we put that back doing the job it was doing before?"

"I'll do it. You grab the printout and check that shelf for an envelope or folder."

"Yes, ma'am." He saluted and crossed the room to the printer. He gathered up the papers that contained what was gibberish for most but pure gold for them. The printout was useless without the code and the code was useless without the printout, but together they told a story of corruption, deceit, betrayal and death—he'd protect both the code and the printout with his life.

GRAY CHOMPED DOWN on the last bite of the taco from the Indian taco place Jerrica had dragged him to.

She dabbed his chin with a napkin. "I can tell you hated it."

"Pretty good for tofu and other healthy junk." He shook the paper bag next to him on the counter. "Are you sure Amit's gonna like this?"

Jerrica slid from her stool and wedged a hand on her hip. "He's a vegetarian."

"A buddy of mine in Delta Force is Indian, and I can assure you he's not a vegetarian."

"If he's in Delta Force, I'm pretty sure he's no pacifist, either."

"At the end of all this, Amit's not going to be a pacifist. If he's going to continue in this line of work, he'd better start packing heat."

Jerrica snatched the bag from the counter. "Maybe he will."

They made it back to Jerrica's apartment building not far from the Indian taco stand on the Lower East Side by the same method they'd used before.

Gray didn't take a breath until they'd reached Jerrica's front door. As they eased it open, they faced Amit, bruised and battered, pointing a gun in their general direction.

Gray poked Jerrica in the back. "What did I tell you?"

"It's just us. Are you all right?" She held out the bag. "We brought you lunch from Goa Taco."

Amit's shoulders dropped. "I slept most of the morning. I feel weak. Maybe the food will help."

"Do you want me to bring it to you in bed?"

"I'll try eating it here." Amit sank to the sofa, the gun still attached to his hand.

"I'll take that, Amit." Gray reached down and loosened the gun from Amit's stiff fingers. "You're going to feel a lot better when we tell you our news."

"I'm ready for some good news—more good news. Kelly's friend messaged me back. Kelly's on her way to Boston—no questions asked."

"That's a relief." Jerrica returned to the living room, two messy tacos on a plate and a glass of water clutched in her other hand. "Do you need more meds?"

"Just some ibuprofen." He held up a trembling hand. "No more stuff to knock me out. I'm groggy enough."

Gray sat in a chair across from Amit and pulled Jerrica's backpack into his lap. Reaching into the pack, he said, "We printed out a chunk of what was coming through on the database you hacked."

Amit swallowed a bit of taco and choked, his dark eyes wide. "Print? You printed out something, Jerrica?"

"I know. Not standard procedure, but we have a code to decipher and the means to do it." She held out her cupped hand containing two gelcaps.

"You're kidding." Amit wiped his nose with the back of his hand and dropped the pills into his mouth.

"Denver sent the code to me, hoping you guys would have something I could apply it to…and you did. We've already deciphered a few words, so I know we're on the right track."

"And…" Jerrica perched on the sofa next to Amit "…I got a meet message from Kiera."

Amit said, "She must have something important to communicate to you if she wants to see you in person."

"I just hope it's not that they've also been compromised." She dropped a paper towel on Amit's thigh.

He grabbed her hand before she could pull it away. "Have you heard from Olaf yet?"

Gray's jaw tightened as he waited for Jerrica's answer. She hadn't told him she'd contacted Olaf, but of course Dreadworm's founder would have to know if his organization had been compromised.

"I haven't heard from him." She shrugged and wrested her hand from Amit's hold. "He probably wants to keep a low profile. Can you blame him? If the Feds ever catch up to him, they're going to arrest him."

Gray plopped the folder on the coffee table. "And you, too. Aren't you guys worried about arrest? It's not just Olaf who's under the gun."

"If we can help thwart a terrorist attack and save a Delta Force major, we might just be able to talk ourselves out of federal prison." Amit nudged the folder on the table with his toe.

"I wouldn't hold your breath." Gray gathered up the papers. "Should I spread these out on the kitchen table?"

"That's probably the best place." Jerrica beat him there and cleared off a vase of colorful flowers and a few dead petals. She pushed aside a candle and stacked the four woven place mats on the edge of the table. "I'm going to put my laptop over here, too. I can probably write a program that will do the decoding for us, so we don't have to match letter for letter."

Gray shook his head. "I'm in awe."

Amit grabbed the arm of the sofa and staggered to his feet. "I was using your computer in the bedroom. Hope that's okay."

"No problem." She waved her hand at Amit. "Sit down. I'll get it."

When she left the room, Gray sat on the arm of

the sofa next to Amit. "Have you ever met Kiera before? Do you even know what she looks like?"

"African-American woman. Small but muscular." Amit held a hand at his shoulder. "Braids about down to here."

"So, if a tall white woman with short hair shows up, we're probably in trouble."

"What are you two whispering about?" Jerrica strode past them and plugged in her laptop at the kitchen table.

"Gray was just asking about Kiera."

Jerrica glanced up from the laptop and puffed a strand of hair from her eyes. "She communicated with me via the message board. This meeting is legit."

"You thought the text Amit sent you was legit, too." Gray pushed up from the sofa and planted himself at the table.

"Cell phones can be stolen. Nobody knows about this message board."

"Except the four of you...and Olaf."

Amit raised a hand. "Leave me out of it. I swear, I didn't reveal anything when they had me. I'm not saying I wouldn't have caved once they got me to their torture chamber, but those cops saved me."

"I'm allowed to be suspicious." Gray flipped open the file and brought up the code on his phone. "I'm going to try to decipher this first line."

Jerrica grabbed the back of his chair. "Before you start, Sherlock, can you send that code to my email address?"

"Is it safe?"

"My email is encrypted. Only I could break into that." She winked at him.

"Okay, here it comes. The subject is a recipe for buttercream frosting."

Jerrica rolled her eyes. "Anyone who knows me would spot that as a fake right away. Go ahead."

Gray emailed her the attachment Major Denver had forwarded to him and the code wheel, and then grabbed a sharpened pencil. Above each letter in the database transcript, he wrote in the corresponding letter from the code.

After one minute, he squinted at his handiwork. "Houston, we have a problem."

"What's wrong?" Jerrica asked.

"There's another layer to this code." He drilled the tip of the pencil into the stack of papers. "It's not a simple substitution."

"But we did a spot check and it worked. The matched-up letters spelled out real words instead of this gibberish."

"Now it's a different kind of gibberish, featuring real words this time, but words that don't make any sense together." He picked up the first sheet of the paper. "How about this? Eagle Scout has landed, but he didn't bring the bubble gum."

"So, if someone does get the code like we just did, he…or she would still be in the dark. A random search for Denver or sarin gas or Times Square would not yield any results." Jerrica folded one leg beneath her.

Across the room, Amit choked. "They're planning to release sarin gas in Times Square?"

Jerrica clicked her tongue. "Relax over there. That was just an example."

"But you know it's sarin gas and you're pretty sure it's New York, aren't you?"

"Gray had some previous intelligence from his Delta Force team and we already knew one of the code words for sarin, but we need hard facts to nail this down." Jerrica tapped the top of her laptop. "I'm going to get going on a program to at least translate the code to real words. We can work on what those words mean, later."

Gray nodded, but his insides tightened. He didn't know how many laters they had. Denver had gone AWOL almost six months ago, betrayed, set up and forced to go on the run due to information he was going to get from a source in Afghanistan. That plan he was investigating must be close to fruition.

"I have a dumb question." Amit gasped as he struggled to rise from the sofa. "Isn't your father Senator Grayson Prescott?"

Gray shot a sideways glance at Jerrica. "He is."

"Why don't you take all of this to him? You trust your own father, don't you?"

A muscled twitched at the corner of Gray's mouth. "I trust him, but he's part of the system. He's former military himself. He's never going to believe those around him, seemingly dedicated to the same goals as he is, may be actively working against those goals undercover. And if I tell him I'm working with Dreadworm, he'll do his duty. Jerrica…both of you…could be in danger of arrest. I'm not going to take that chance—even with my father."

"I get it." Amit limped to the kitchen and held up a hand to stop Jerrica who'd jumped to his aid. "I have to start moving around by myself. I plan to join Kelly in Boston as soon as I can…unless you two need me."

"You've done enough." Gray leaned back in the chair and crossed his arms behind his head. "But don't rush it. You lost a lot of blood and if your ribs aren't broken, they're bruised."

"I'll give it a day or two, and I'll help however I can while I'm here." Amit rubbed the back of his skull. "I sure wish Olaf would check in with us."

"Seems like you two have already been doing most of the heavy lifting without Olaf."

"Olaf *is* Dreadworm." Amit turned his dark gaze on Gray. "You don't like Olaf, do you?"

"Let's just say, I think he's caused a lot of trouble."

"Gray's always had a thing against Olaf." Jerrica lodged her tongue in the corner of her mouth.

Gray clenched his teeth. He must've been obvious about his jealousy toward Olaf. "I realize if it weren't for Olaf and Dreadworm, we wouldn't even be close to nailing down this plan. So, I'm feeling kind of warm and fuzzy about the guy now."

"That'll be the day." Jerrica clicked a few more keystrokes. "We'd better start getting ready to meet Kiera."

"There's something special you need to do for the meeting?" Gray's *something special* meant bringing a weapon.

"It's kind of silly, but I'll wear a cap with the TV show's logo on it. That's how she'll pick me out."

"You've never met her before?" The uneasiness churned in his gut again.

"I haven't, but Amit has. I know what she looks like, and she has a description of me. It's fine, Gray."

"Then let's get the cap."

GRAY AND JERRICA set out again, exiting from the building next door. If anyone was watching Jerrica's building, maybe they'd believe they all relocated. Maybe they *should* all relocate.

If Gray hoped to identify any of the government moles, he and Jerrica would have to plan a trip to DC, anyway. And what could be safer than a sitting US senator's home in North Arlington?

His mother was always coming up to DC to throw parties, and their gathering for Memorial Day was legendary with all the movers and shakers in attendance. Dad was always trying to foist him on the political powerbrokers. Maybe it was time for him to show interest.

"We're taking the subway." Jerrica hooked a finger in his belt loop and tugged.

"I'm an expert now. Washington Square Park?" Gray planted himself in front of a map on the wall in the subway station and studied the multicolored lines crisscrossing Manhattan.

He placed his hand on the small of Jerrica's back. "This way."

Gray successfully got them to their location and as they climbed the stairs to fresh air, he tucked his sunglasses into his pocket. He hadn't bothered with a disguise, but Jerrica had that silly hat with the ghoulish logo pulled down to her eyebrows.

As they entered the park, Gray's muscles tensed and his gaze darted around the open space. A kid screamed, causing a hitch in his step.

Jerrica patted his arm. "I know how you feel."

Did she? Gray slipped his hand into his jacket pocket and caressed his gun. Jerrica, usually so careful and on edge, almost had a spring in her step as she approached a bench.

She must trust Olaf so absolutely that she trusted everyone around him. If Olaf had hand-picked Kiera, she must be golden.

Jerrica settled on the bench facing the street. "I'll see her coming, and she'll see me."

Gray remained standing and scanned the students with their backpacks, the couples on a stroll to somewhere else and a couple of transients looking for a handout. "I'm going to leave you here to meet Kiera while I play scout."

"Do you want me to send up a smoke signal or something when I see her?" Jerrica crossed one leg over the other and immediately began her nervous habit of kicking her foot back and forth.

The gesture gave him some comfort that she was taking this meeting seriously.

"No. I'm sure I'll know her when I see her—gauzy red scarf, right?"

"Yes. We shouldn't be long. She'll tell me what she needs to, and we'll part ways. I don't owe her any information, and I don't plan to tell her anything about what Amit and I have going on—just that we've been compromised and to watch out."

"Got it." He squeezed her shoulder and sauntered away to people watch.

A few minutes later, a short African-American woman with long braids, a long skirt and a red scarf hanging loosely over her shoulders shuffled into the park area.

She glanced over her shoulder, and Gray narrowed his eyes and peered behind her for any unusual activity. Maybe nerves had gotten the better of her, too, and she was checking for a tail.

She seemed to be dragging her feet, as if meeting Jerrica was the last thing she wanted to do.

Her head jerked to the side, and she pinned Jerrica with an unrelenting stare. Keeping her focus on Jerrica, Kiera walked toward her as if in a trance.

Gray licked his dry lips. Out of the corner of his eye, he sensed movement and his skin prickled as he watched a previously stationary homeless guy give up his prime spot and mosey toward Jerrica's bench.

Kiera's head shifted slightly toward the transient and the three of them—Jerrica, Kiera and the homeless guy formed a taut triangle that buzzed with electricity.

Gray's head snapped toward Jerrica. Did she sense it?

Her leg kicked back and forth furiously, and she craned her neck like a bird trying to scope out the offerings. She felt something.

The transient picked up the pace, making a beeline toward Jerrica. Kiera waved, keeping

Jerrica's attention focused on her trusted Dread-worm coworker.

Gray's brain clicked with every movement of the two people closing in on Jerrica. As if in slow motion, the homeless man reached into one of his bulging bags, keeping his hand planted inside.

Would he kill both of them, or just Jerrica?

Adrenaline pumped through Gray's system and it felt as if he had springs on the bottom of his shoes as he bounded forward.

Kiera whipped her head around toward him, her braids flying through the air, her eyes wide.

It was enough of a signal to the transient, who didn't even turn around to look at Gray. Instead, his hand emerged from the bag, his fingers wrapped around a gun with a silencer attached. He'd probably never meant to shoot Jerrica from this distance, but his plans had clearly just changed.

So had Gray's.

"Jerrica, take cover!" As Gray shouted, the unmistakable whiz of a bullet zipped through the air.

Gray hoped to God it hadn't found its mark, but he had to keep his eye on the gunman who looked ready to take another shot. Gray steadied his own weapon and leveled it at the fake transient.

Before Gray could get off a shot, the man grabbed a child running past in the confusion.

Using the boy as a shield, the gunman backed out of the park amid the screaming and chaos.

Then his arm rose and he shot Kiera where she stood.

Chapter Eight

The bullet from the silenced gun cut through the air and the pounding in Jerrica's eardrums. Was it aimed at her? At Gray? God, not the boy. She dug her nails into the dirt beneath the bench where she'd taken cover.

As the gunman pushed the little boy and he fell to his knees, Jerrica opened her mouth in a silent scream. She scrambled forward on her belly to reach the boy, who popped up crying but unscathed and ran to his mother's outstretched arms.

Jerrica collapsed. Thank God the boy hadn't been harmed.

"Jerrica, are you hit?" Gray's voice invaded the fog encompassing her head, and she reached out a hand.

"I'm okay. He didn't shoot that child." If she'd had to bear witness to another child dying from a gunshot wound, it would've been almost impossible for her to get to her feet.

Crouching beside her, Gray put his arm around her waist and helped her up. "Kiera wasn't so lucky."

As her boots hit the ground, Jerrica's legs gave way beneath her and she grabbed Gray's arm. She didn't need to, as he'd kept a firm, steadying hold on her.

She peeked over his shoulder at Kiera splayed in the dirt, her braids fanning out around her head as a pool of blood inched its way to the ends of the arc they created.

She turned her face into Gray's shoulder and mumbled against the rough denim of his jacket. "Oh my God. Why?"

"I guess he figured if he couldn't shoot one Dreadworm hacker, he'd shoot another."

"But Kiera had nothing to do with the compromised database." She tugged on his sleeve. "Police."

Gray stroked bits of debris from the hair hanging below her cap. "We don't know anything. We don't know Kiera. We were here taking a stroll."

"What if someone saw you pull out your weapon?" She patted the gun Gray had crammed back into his pocket.

"I doubt anyone noticed, but if someone did, I have a concealed-carry permit. I saw the man had a gun, and I was going to try to take him down. Best to stick with the truth as much as possible."

"Why didn't you?"

"Why didn't I what?" Gray nodded at the cop headed their way.

"Take him down."

"He'd grabbed the boy by the time I could take aim. I'm a pretty good shot, but I'm not going to risk a child's life. You were safe, I had cover and I never thought he'd turn on Kiera."

"Why *did* he shoot her?"

"Shh." Gray hissed in her ear at the officer's approach.

"You folks witness what happened here?"

After introducing himself to the officer, Gray kept his story brief and to the point. Nobody must've noticed his gun because the officer didn't question him about it, and he didn't offer it up.

"Ma'am, what did you see?"

"Not much of anything." Jerrica swept the cap from her head and ran her fingers through her tangled hair. "I saw that the transient had a gun, and my…boyfriend saw it, too. He warned me to take cover, and I did. I had my eyes on the child the man grabbed, so I didn't even realize he'd shot the woman. Is she…?"

"Yes, she's deceased." The cop tapped his pencil against his notebook. "Did he seem to be targeting her? Others said he was walking in the direction of this bench."

Gray cleared his throat. "I'm not sure he was

targeting anyone. He pulled out his weapon, the people who noticed it screamed and started running out of the park or taking cover. He shot the woman. Then he took off."

"Can you give me a description?"

Jerrica held up her hands. "I can't. I didn't get a good look at him."

"I can help with that."

Gray proceeded to give the officer a description of the transient, and both he and Jerrica gave him their names and phone numbers.

"Thanks. We'll be in touch if we need more information, and call us if you remember anything else." The cop tucked his notebook into his pocket, pivoted and then stopped. "It's weird though. You wouldn't think a homeless guy would have a gun with a silencer attached."

"That is strange." Gray draped his arm around Jerrica's shoulders. "Can we leave now?"

"Sure, and thank you for your service, Lieutenant Prescott."

"Thank you for *yours*."

Gray entwined his fingers with Jerrica's and tugged. They left the park, and she didn't even give a parting glance to Kiera's dead body on the ground.

They kept silent for two long blocks, putting as much space as possible between themselves and the park.

Gray pointed ahead to a street glowing with welcoming lights. "Let's get something to eat."

"Should we tell Amit what happened?"

"He doesn't have a phone and even if he did, I'm not sure I trust your device."

"You have your phone. I'll communicate with him through the message board." She stopped in front of a bistro and grabbed the door handle. "Here."

Gray reached above her and pushed open the door. The whoosh of noise and warmth and savory smells cast an immediate spell on Jerrica, luring her inside the buzzing scene.

She closed her eyes. The longing for normality hit her like a sledgehammer. Why now? With everything in her life coming to a head, she sensed an explosion in her future—and she didn't mean the kind the terrorists had planned.

"Two?" The hostess appeared before them, and Gray nodded.

"We'll take the bar if we have to."

"We just cleared a table by the kitchen." The hostess tried to keep her gaze from wandering over Gray's body but failed.

Jerrica couldn't blame her, but she didn't have to like it. She stepped between the hostess and her view. "That's fine."

The hostess eked out a tight smile and spun around, crooking her finger. "Follow me."

Gray rested a hand on Jerrica's hip and leaned close. "It's crowded in here."

"A good spot in case we were followed, don't you think?"

"We weren't followed." He dug his fingertips into the swell of her hip. "I made sure of that."

The hostess seated them, and Gray slid one of the menus she'd left toward Jerrica. "Please tell me there's something more than veggie stuff here."

"This isn't a vegetarian place. I think they even have—" she whispered "—burgers."

Jerrica grabbed the edge of the menu to flip it open with a hand that still trembled.

Gray didn't miss a thing. He covered her fingers with his own. "You're sure you're okay?"

"Still shaken. If you hadn't warned me to take a dive, I'd be as dead as Kiera—unless he killed her because he couldn't kill me." She finally opened the menu and stared at the words blurring in front of her.

"I think he always intended to kill Kiera."

"You think he made her, too, and intercepted our communication?"

A busboy set two glasses of water down. As soon as he left, Gray reached across the table again.

"Jerrica." Gray placed his hands flat across her menu. "I think Kiera's the one who gave you up.

She tried to set you up for him. He must've had something on her."

"No." She took a gulp of water and put down the glass harder than she'd intended. "Why would she do that?"

"Being in military intelligence, I can think of several reasons why." He held up his hand and ticked off his fingers. "Someone threatened her, threatened her family, had something on her for blackmail, paid her off. The reasons are endless."

They ended their conversation again as the waiter approached. Gray ordered a burger and fries and she ordered a veggie burger, although she had little appetite for anything now.

She dug her elbows into the table and buried her chin in her palm. "I can't believe she'd do that."

"Why? You didn't know her. You'd never even seen her before tonight."

"Because she's Dreadworm. Olaf vetted us all thoroughly."

"Even the great Olaf can make mistakes." Gray rolled his eyes.

"I suppose, but that puts him in danger, too."

"The next question is, who outed Kiera?" Gray steepled his fingers and peered at her over the apex. "Where did it all start? If Kiera had to tell them about you and Amit, who told them about her? Who's her coworker? Cedar?"

"Yeah, Cedar."

Gray raised his eyebrows and his lips quirked into a grin.

"Cedar grew up on a commune. You don't want to know his brothers' names."

"You're right. I don't." Gray traced the edge of his water glass. "You seem to know more about him than Kiera."

"About the same. Kiera's father was one of the founding members of the Black Panthers. She has a son who attends Columbia." She sniffled and swirled the ice in her glass before taking a sip. "I know a few salient facts about them."

"The facts that make them ripe for working at Dreadworm."

"I suppose you could say that. What's your point?"

"My point is that Olaf chose wisely. He must've recruited most of you. It's not like you went on an internet job board."

"Food's here." She wanted to cut off this conversation about Olaf and how she knew him. She poked at her burger. "Mustard, please."

The waiter answered, "Absolutely. Anything else?"

"Actually, I'd like a beer. Jerrica? I think we both could use one."

"Sure. Make it two, and I'll have whatever he's having."

Gray made a selection from the beer menu and then doused his fries with ketchup. "Don't worry. I'm not going to drink to the point where I can't get us back to your place safely."

"I know that." She held her hand out over the table and it was mostly steady. "I'm almost calm."

"How do we reach Cedar?"

"Ugh, I knew that was going to be your next question." She thanked the waiter for the mustard and squirted some on her bun. "We have our own message board with another TV show."

"Then it's time we either warn him or kill him."

Jerrica flicked a napkin in his face.

"I'm just kidding—sort of. For all we know, he could be dead already."

"Okay, just stop." She pointed a knife at him. "I sent out the SOS to Cedar, too, but he didn't respond."

"Even if he does, you're not going to any more secret meetings. Communicate with him via the message board, and that's it." He picked up a fry and waved it at her. "I'm not allowing you to be an easy target again."

"Once Cedar sees the news and learns Kiera is dead, he's either going to contact me or he's going to run."

The waiter placed their beers in front of them.

Gray finished chewing his french fry and then took a long pull from his mug.

"I needed that." He clinked his glass with hers. "Here's to finding out who's exposing Dreadworm…and why."

"And why." Jerrica took a sip of beer through the thick head of foam and closed her eyes as the alcohol sent warm, soothing waves to her frazzled nerve endings.

Gray interrupted her happy place. "I think we know the why. They know Dreadworm has compromised their clandestine database, and they want to keep you out before you can discover anything of substance…or turn it over to someone who can."

"I know." Jerrica opened her eyes and nibbled at the edge of her veggie burger, her appetite still lying in the dirt with Kiera's body. "But that's Amit and I. Kiera and Cedar have no knowledge of this database. Why go after them?"

"To get to you. If Amit didn't rat you out, and it doesn't sound like he did, and you didn't give him up, how did these people know where to find the two of you? How'd they know to pick up Amit's trail at that party? How'd they find out where you live? Kiera led one of them straight to you. They got to her somehow, turned her somehow—and killed her when she'd served her purpose."

Jerrica dropped her burger. "This time he was

willing to kill me. What changed? The first attempt on Amit and me was abduction. That guy with the gun in the park looked intent on murder...not kidnapping."

"We don't know what he would've done. Maybe he squeezed off the shot to wound you and would've taken you captive after that. Kiera he had no use for."

"If Amit and I are dead, our programs die with us and we won't have the opportunity to send anything to Olaf."

Gray glanced up sharply from his plate. "Is that what you intend to do? Send this info to Olaf?"

"W-we always do."

"Have you told him about this, yet?"

"How could we?" Jerrica wrapped her hands around the mug, sweating beads of moisture. "We didn't really know what we had until you showed up with the code."

"You knew you had a black ops database inside the government."

"I knew that, and I communicated it to Olaf. Whether or not Amit did the same, I'm not sure."

Gray swiped a napkin across the lower half of his face. "Dreadworm really is a case of the right hand not knowing what the left is doing."

"Olaf designed it that way. It cuts down on the type of situation we find ourselves in now. I was surprised that Olaf even told us about each other and that Amit and I work in the same office." Jerrica traced a finger around the base of her mug. "Look at us now."

"Strange."

"We have to get back to Amit. I have to tell him what happened. If he's watching TV or going through news sites online, he may already know. He's going to be worried."

"You barely touched your dinner."

She poked at her burger on the plate. "I suppose I can take it home, and Amit can have the uneaten half."

"Get the waiter over here while I finish my food—and my beer." Gray dug into his burger while she waved at the server.

"Can I get this to go, please, and the check?"

"Sure. Anything else?"

Jerrica shook her head. "Not unless you have an armored car."

"Excuse me?"

"Just the check, thanks."

Gray studied her over his mug. "Let's take a taxi back. We can get dropped off around the corner and come through the other building."

"I guess we can do that. It'll be safer."

Gray polished off the last of his fries by dragging them through the puddle of ketchup on his plate and popping them in his mouth. "With your money, you could hire a car and a bodyguard."

"I could hire a car and a driver, but I already have my bodyguard." She grabbed his wrist. "I never said thank you for saving my life."

"I didn't do much. I was too slow. I should've shot him."

"For all my security measures and heightened senses, I didn't even notice the guy coming at me. I didn't see the gun until you yelled—saving my life." She squeezed his arm. "Can you imagine the mess if you'd shot him? The police? The questions?"

"I would've been within my rights. He had a gun out." Gray crumpled his napkin and tossed it onto the table. "I could've taken out the bastard. Sent a message."

"It didn't work out that way, but we're both safe." She put her hands together as if in prayer and pressed the tips of her fingers against her lips to stifle the sob bubbling from her throat. "Kiera. Her son."

"These people are out of control, Jerrica. Scares the hell out of me. They're desperate."

"And that's just how we want them. They know we're in the database. Imagine how they'd react if they knew we had the first part of the code to decipher their gibberish."

He hunched his shoulders. "I hope they never find that out. As long as they think you're scrabbling around with meaningless words, maybe this group, whatever and whoever it is, won't bring their full forces down on you—because those forces must be awful if they can set up a man like Denver and keep dismissing all evidence that would exonerate him."

"Okay, now you've really ruined my evening. Let's head back to my place and check on Amit."

After settling the check, they stepped onto the street and walked a half a block before grabbing a taxi. Gray sat sideways the entire ride back to her neighborhood to keep an eye out the rear window. Occasionally, he'd tell the puzzled driver to take a quick right or left.

When the taxi pulled up to the curb around the block from her apartment building, Gray leaned over and whispered in her ear. "Didn't notice anyone following us."

He paid the driver, and they turned down the alley that led to the building next to hers.

By default, Jerrica stuck close to the wall and the shadows, and Gray gravitated toward her, matching her step for stealthy step. Even with Gray's solid presence beside her, the cold that had seeped under her skin, and had receded only with the beer and the company, crept back, needling her flesh.

Gray curled an arm around her waist, fitting her against his body, as if sensing her unease. Or maybe he felt it, too.

"Do we need a key for this door?"

"Not this one. Remember, it leads to the stairwell and the two doors—one leading to each building." She dragged her keychain from her pocket. "I *do* have a key for that door."

Gray reached around her and pushed down on the handle. The squeak it made had her grinding her back teeth. He eased open the door wide enough to accommodate his bulky frame but no more.

She tripped in ahead of him, pinching the key in her fingers. She waited until Gray pulled the door closed behind them, then pivoted to the door that led to her building's basement.

The yellow light from the bare bulb above them cast a weak glow over the metal door. Suddenly Jerrica gasped and threw out her hands in front of her. The icy prickles she'd felt in the alley stabbed the back of her neck as she stretched out her fingers to trace over the chalk letters scribbled on the door to her building.

In a voice that quavered just a little, she read aloud, "It's Olaf."

Chapter Nine

Gray caught Jerrica around the shoulders as she listed to one side. He narrowed his eyes as he read the message on the door. "What the hell does that mean? What's Olaf?"

"Cedar wrote this."

"Cedar?" He asked as if he knew more than one Cedar. "How do you know that?"

She leveled a finger at a drawing of a tree near the corner of the message. "That's his signature. Cedar, tree. Get it?"

"Okay, but why did he leave this message and what does it mean? What's he trying to say about Olaf?"

"I'm not sure, but I don't want to stand here all night while we figure it out." She shoved the key in the lock and pushed on the door.

"Wait." Gray grabbed the edge of the door. "Let's get rid of it. I'm pretty sure he meant that for your eyes only."

"If you're getting rid of it, I want proof that it

existed." She dug her phone from her pocket and took a picture of the words. "It's all yours."

Gray erased the chalk with the sleeve of his jacket, and prodded her through the open door. "I just hope nobody else saw it."

"Who would see it? Nobody knows about this entrance into my building, except the residents, and I'm not even sure some of them know you can go from one building to the other."

Gray covered his nose and mouth with his hand as they made their way through the foul-smelling basement. "How did Cedar know about the connected buildings?"

"He dropped something off for me one night, and I told him about it because I didn't want him coming to my front door. I guess he remembered, and realized now is the time to lay low."

They maneuvered their way back to Jerrica's place, and Gray tensed his muscles while she released the locks. He didn't know what to expect on the other side.

Jerrica swung open the door and sang out. "It's just us."

Amit met them from the other side of a gun. "What the hell happened out there?"

"Put the gun down, Amit." Gray raised his hands. "We're the good guys, remember?"

"Just taking precautions after what happened in Washington Square Park." He placed the weapon on the coffee table, and then collapsed on the sofa as if the effort of raising and pointing that gun had been too much for him. "That was you, right? The shooting? The dead body? That was Kiera, wasn't it? I read a report online."

Jerrica sat beside him and put a hand on his bouncing knee. "It was. Our meeting was blown. Some guy with a gun, dressed as a transient, crashed our party."

"Oh, God." Amit pressed his palm against his forehead. "Was it like last time? Did he try to abduct you…or did he want to kill you this time?"

"We're not sure." Gray scooped up the gun from the table. "He was there panhandling when we got to the park. Kiera walked up, spotted Jerrica and made her move, but she looked scared. It raised my hackles—even more than they already were. That's when I noticed the homeless guy walking in a trajectory toward Jerrica."

"I was so focused on Kiera, I didn't even notice him. Gray shouted out a warning when he saw the guy's gun, and I dove under the bench."

"How did Kiera end up getting shot?" Amit's dark skin had a decidedly pale cast to it.

"When Gray foiled the gunman's attack on him, the guy grabbed a child as a shield and then shot Kiera on his way out of the park."

"The kid?" Amit's eyes bugged out like a cartoon character's.

Gray answered, "The boy's fine. You didn't read about anyone else getting hurt, did you?"

"No." Amit wiped his brow with the back of his hand and repeated his question. "Was the man going to shoot Jerrica or abduct her at gunpoint?"

"We're not sure." Gray snatched the cap from Jerrica's head and kissed her messy hair. "I wasn't gonna wait to find out."

"How was the meeting compromised? Do you think Kiera ratted you out, Jerrica?"

"You're asking all the same questions we did. You know about as much as we do now about what happened in the park, but there's more." She slid a quick glance at Gray, and he nodded.

Amit was in the thick of it as much as they were.

Jerrica licked her lips as she pulled out her phone. "When we got back here, Cedar had left a message in chalk on the door to the building's basement."

Amit dragged a pillow into his lap as if for security and hugged it against his bruised ribs. "A message? Cedar?"

Jerrica tapped her phone and brought up the photo she'd taken of the words on the door. She zoomed in. "Look."

"There's his stupid tree. It had to be him, right? Unless someone knows how he signs off." Amit dug his fingers into the pillow in his lap. "How'd he know where you live, and how'd he know about the alley entrance?"

"He came through my building that way once when he delivered something to me—that was even before I was really being followed."

"What is Cedar talking about? Olaf? What about Olaf? What does Cedar mean that Olaf is *it*?"

"Slow down." Jerrica grabbed her bag of food from the table. "Have you eaten anything? I brought you my leftover veggie burger."

Amit downed half the sandwich before he came up for air. "Cedar must be communicating with you with chalk messages because he's afraid to use the message board. You used the message board with Kiera and look what happened."

Gray sat on the edge of the chair across from Amit and Jerrica. "Is there any way someone could've found out or figured out the message board thing on his own?"

Both Amit and Jerrica shook their heads in unison.

Jerrica said, "There's no way. There's no rhyme or reason to the message board or our user names. It's not something someone could figure out. Someone might guess the fan boards as a mode of secret communication—I'm sure it's done all the time—but there are hundreds of these boards, hundreds of shows, thousands of users with all kinds of screen monikers."

Gray rubbed his chin. "Could someone have broken into—or whatever you call that—Kiera's computer? You're sure nobody got into yours?"

"We sweep our computers daily for threats. I'm sure Cedar and Kiera do the same—it's part of our training." Jerrica stuffed the empty foam container into the bag and pushed up from the sofa. On her way to the kitchen, she called over her shoulder. "And after the break-in, I did a thorough scan. Nobody was in my computer."

Amit put a hand to the back of his head and toyed with the bandage. "If nobody compromised the computers, and I believe Jerrica's right about that, then somebody compromised Kiera. You said she looked nervous. She knew someone would be there. She knew what was going down, but she probably hadn't counted on getting killed herself."

"And if they got to Kiera, who's to say they haven't gotten to Cedar, too?" Jerrica returned to the living room and hovered behind Amit.

He turned and stared at her. "Are you questioning me now? You searched me when I collapsed on your doorstep, barely able to take a breath, and didn't find any bugs on me. Is that what you think?"

"Why would you come here?" Jerrica folded her arms. "We're not besties or anything."

"Excuse me for thinking you might have a heart beneath the computer chips." Amit tried to rise in a huff but only made it halfway before falling back against the cushion.

"Hang on." Gray sliced a hand through the air. "Don't start cannibalizing each other."

Jerrica dropped her hands to Amit's shoulders and he flinched beneath her touch. "I'm sorry, Amit. I don't think for a minute you're the Dreadworm mole. I'm just jumpy. Can you blame me? I just saw a woman die in front of me, a child grabbed as a hostage."

Jerrica's voice hung in the room, and she flushed. She'd never use her past to garner sympathy, but there it was. That scene in the park must've brought back memories for her. She'd witnessed the murder of her mother and her brother. Her father had died a fiery death when the FBI had blown up the place where Jimmy James had kept his stash of weapons. Jerrica didn't even have her father's body to bury. She'd had to ID him through a necklace he'd always worn.

Amit must've heard her tone, too. He grabbed Jerrica's fingers and said, "I'm sorry. You had every right to suspect me, especially as I was stupid enough to get caught and then even more stupid to potentially lead my abductors to your place. But you know what?"

"What?" She blinked her eyes rapidly and swiped her hand across her nose.

"Even though we're not…besties, I came to you because you're badass, and that was even before I knew you'd partnered with a Delta Force badass."

Gray clapped his hands to defuse the awkwardness. "Now that you've eliminated each other as suspects…again…let's get back to Cedar's message. What is he trying to tell you about Olaf? Has Olaf gotten back to your SOS, Jerrica?"

"No, but that's not unusual. Sometimes it takes him days to respond."

"Cedar left that message after Kiera's murder. Would Olaf have any reason to want Kiera dead?"

"What? No." Jerrica shot up, pulling back her shoulders. "Olaf wouldn't harm one of his own people."

Amit traced the lump beneath his eye. "Are you sure? What if he found out Kiera had betrayed you?"

"How could he find out that quickly? Gray and I didn't even realize Kiera had betrayed me until the so-called transient pulled out his gun—and I'm still not sure she did double-cross me. How could Olaf have known that?"

"Maybe he saw something before. The man may be in hiding, but he knows and sees more than most people on the ground—us included." Hunching forward, Amit grabbed the arm of the sofa.

"Where do you think you're going?" Jerrica circled the couch to stand in front of her captive guest.

"I need to get up and move before I sink into that sofa. Do you have any tea? I'll make myself a cup."

Jerrica held out her hand, Amit grabbed it and she helped him to his feet. "Get me one, too, please."

Amit straightened slowly, pressing one arm across his midsection. "You want one, Gray?"

"Me? Tea?" Gray poked a finger at his own chest. "No, thanks, but if she's got a beer in there, I'll take that."

"I have a couple of bottles." She smacked a hand against the pocket of the jacket she hadn't removed when they walked into the apartment. "My phone."

"Someone's calling?" Gray's pulse ticked up. "Could it be Cedar following up?"

Jerrica squinted at her phone's display. "I don't know. It's a message notification. Someone responded to my message on the zombie-show board, after my original message."

Amit clanged a pot and then limped out of the kitchen. "That can't be. That's Kiera's board."

Gray circled his finger in the air. "Do what you have to do."

Jerrica dropped to her knees in front of the laptop Amit had left on the coffee table. She tapped on the keyboard. "I'll check it."

Amit perched on the edge of the sofa behind Jerrica, and Gray crouched beside her.

She brought up the message board and scrolled down to the thread that contained her post. "It's a new message under Kiera's user name, Deadgirl."

Amit choked. "She must've had a premonition."

Gray rubbed his eyes as the small letters kept blurring in and out of focus. "What does it say, Jerrica?"

"It says, 'I think the Forest is a better setting. They could do stories for the eleven new characters in the Forest.'"

"Okay, what the hell does that mean?" Gray trailed his fingers through his short hair.

"The Forest is Times Square, and she wants to meet at eleven o'clock. The meeting place is the discount ticket kiosk."

"She? She's dead, Jerrica." Gray jumped as the tea kettle whistled. "You're not meeting anyone tonight."

Amit hobbled back to the kitchen. "I agree with Gray. Looks like the impossible happened and someone figured out our communication system—or Kiera told someone."

"That's impossible, and why would Kiera tell anyone? She gave them what they wanted, leading them to me. There would be no reason for her to reveal our method of communication. The people who got to her figured I'd be dead or captured by now. They wouldn't have thought they'd need a way to communicate with me going forward."

Her jaw formed a hard line, and Gray's stomach sank. "You're going to Times Square, aren't you?"

She grabbed the cap she'd discarded on the sofa and bunched it up in her fist. "Broadway tickets, anyone?"

GRAY HAD CONVINCED her to keep the cap in her pocket until they could figure out what was what and who was who. He'd also convinced her to take a taxi to Times Square, but he hadn't convinced her not to go.

As he slid into the taxi beside her, he said, "Why would Cedar send you two messages? He scrawled one on the door. Why send another through a message board, Kiera's message board?"

"I don't know, but keep your eye out for a scraggly dude with shoulder-length hair, maybe a man bun, and a backpack. Cedar always carries a backpack."

"In Times Square? Easy." He bent his head close to hers and whispered. "It's the ones we can't identify that worry me."

The taxi crawled through the traffic until Jerrica couldn't stand it anymore. She rapped on the divider. "You can pull over up here."

As the car rolled to a stop, she jumped out while Gray handed the driver some cash.

She elbowed Gray in the ribs. "Don't look so worried. If someone were following us, he would stand out like a sore thumb now, right? He'd be getting out of his taxi, too."

Gray walked backward for a few steps, and then turned around. "Nobody's following us—they're probably waiting at the ticket booth instead."

"This time I'm not going to be a sitting duck." A few blocks later, Jerrica grabbed Gray's hand and pulled him across the street toward the pedestrian area of Times Square. "We can hang out behind the bleachers and have a clear view of the kiosk."

They stationed themselves at the corner of the stands where people scattered, taking seats to watch the carnival unfold before them.

Jerrica hoped to God she and Gray wouldn't be providing any more excitement. A figure moved through the crowd wearing a cap like the one in her pocket. Jerrica's heart skipped a beat.

She plucked at Gray's sleeve. "I see someone with the cap. Three o'clock from the Spider-Man character."

Gray moved closer to her and tucked an arm around her waist. "Skinny black kid with the ear-buds?"

"Yes."

"No man bun, no backpack. That's not Cedar, is it?"

"Cedar's a white guy. That is definitely not Cedar."

"Then we leave. If you don't know who that is, we get the hell out of here."

"Even if we can take him in and get some intel out of him?"

"Take him in? Here?" Gray's eyes widened. "That's not gonna happen."

"Wait." Jerrica pulled the cap from her pocket. "I know him."

"Are you sure?"

"I'm pretty sure, and it would make total sense right now."

"*Pretty sure* is not good enough when it comes to your safety, Jerrica." Gray slipped his fingers into the waistband of her jeans from behind as if to hold her back. "Who do you *think* it is?"

"That's Russell Cramer—Kiera's son."

She moved forward and jerked to a stop as Gray pulled on her pants.

"Wait. If Kiera was compromised, how do we know they didn't send out her son to lure you in again?"

"Really? He just lost his mother." She twisted away from Gray and plunged into the crowd as she pulled the cap onto her head.

With Gray dogging her steps, she approached Russell and touched his elbow. "I like your cap."

He jumped and spun around, his fists clenched.

Gray moved between them smoothly and growled through his teeth. "You touch her and I'll flatten you."

The young man clutched his stomach and spluttered. "A-are you Jerrica?"

"Yes." She slipped the cap from her head and shoved it back into her pocket. No sense in announcing to the world that she and Russell shared some kind of connection. She dropped her gaze to the skinny arm pressed against his belly. "Are you okay, Russell?"

"Not really." He swiped at a bead of sweat rolling down his face and missed. "You know my name?"

"I do. Let's talk."

"Did anyone follow you?" Gray had shifted to the side, but his body radiated menace and it had poor Russell quaking in his sneakers.

"No. After posting that message, I snuck out of the…hospital." His voice caught on a sob. "I left through the loading dock. If anyone was watching the hospital entrance or the waiting room, they never would've seen me."

Jerrica felt a stab of pain. Russell had just lost his mother, and he wasn't much older than she'd been when she lost hers. But Kiera must've taught him well.

"Sorry, man." Gray patted down Russell's thin frame anyway. "Let's head to that fast food place and talk."

Russell's grief had obviously taken a toll on him. As they crossed the street to the hamburger place, he lurched and tripped beside them. Gray had to grab his arm a few times to keep him upright.

They squeezed into the restaurant, and Jerrica grabbed a table with Russell while Gray ordered some food and drinks to buy their spot.

Jerrica patted Russell's hand. "Are you hungry?"

"Not really. No. I can't eat." Russell's head dropped and he kept it down until Gray returned with a tray full of paper-wrapped burgers and empty cups.

After he placed the tray on the table, he held up the cups. "Do you want something to drink?"

"Ginger ale if they have it. My stomach feels

bad." Russell slouched back and for the first time, Jerrica saw that the whites of his eyes had a yellow cast to them.

She sucked in a breath. "You don't look well, Russell."

"That's because I—I've been poisoned."

Chapter Ten

Jerrica put a hand to her throat. "You need to get help."

"No." Russell pounded a weak fist against the table. "I can't tell anyone. They said not to tell."

"Who, Russell?" Gray hunched over the table, squeezing the paper cups in his hand. "Who poisoned you? Was it to get to your mother?"

"Of course. Someone poisoned me and when I came home sick, a man and a woman dropped in on my mother and threatened her. I-I didn't understand that much because whatever they gave me made me fade in and out. I just know they threatened her."

"How'd you make it here? How'd you get to the hospital?" Jerrica folded her arms on the table, her fingers digging into her biceps.

"The man and my mother left. The woman stayed behind with me. I think she got a call or a text, and then she gave me a shot. As soon as I started feeling better, she left, but not before she warned me not to tell anyone anything."

"And yet here you are." A muscle ticked at the corner of Gray's jaw.

Jerrica shot him a look from the corner of her eye. She was supposed to be the cold one. "The shot was supposed to make you better? Counter-act the poison?"

"Yeah, but how can I trust them? They killed my mom." Russell rubbed his eyes. "I still feel bad, but I'd recovered enough to answer the phone when the police called to tell me my mom had been shot in Washington Square Park."

"Eat something. It might help you feel better." Gray shoved a burger toward Russell. "How did you know to post that message on the fan board?"

"Before the man took Mom away, she tucked a note in the waistband of my sweats when they weren't looking. After the woman left and I could move, I pulled it out. She left instructions that if anything happened to her, I was supposed to post that message on the board and to come to Times Square at eleven o'clock." He shook his head and pulled off the cap. "I thought it was some kind of joke until the cops called."

Jerrica traced a pattern on the table top. "She wanted me to know that she hadn't betrayed me."

"Betrayed you? What's going on? My mom

was a computer programmer. I don't understand any of this."

"Eat." Gray held up the cups. "I'm going to get you some water."

As Gray walked away, Russell peeled the waxy paper from the burger. "Did you work with my mom?"

"We worked at the same place—Dreadworm."

Russell choked and went into a coughing fit.

Gray returned with the drinks and pushed a cup of water toward Russell. "Is he okay?"

"I just told him his mother and I worked for Dreadworm."

"Why would you tell him that? You might be endangering his life even more."

"He deserves to know. Nobody has seen us together. They have no idea Kiera left her son that note, and I've told you before that message board is secure. They probably think he's still at the hospital filling out forms. Why would they follow him, anyway?"

"To make sure he doesn't go to the police."

Russell had recovered and gulped down some water. "I'm not going to the police. I thought about it after I found out that they killed my mom, but then I figured they could get to me if they wanted to. They poisoned me without my even knowing about it."

"Going to the police would be pointless, Russell. The people who poisoned you and killed your mother are not going to be caught or stopped by the police."

Toying with the burger, Russell asked, "Dreadworm? You mean that Olaf guy?"

"Yes, your mother was a hacker for Dreadworm, as I am. My coworker and I hacked into a secret database. Someone found out, and they're trying to get us to stop."

"By killing my mom?"

"They used your mother to get to me. She allowed it because she was trying to protect you, and now we're going to make sure you stay safe."

"How are you going to do that?" Russell looked around wildly. "Nobody's safe."

Jerrica sucked in her bottom lip. Another paranoid conspiracy theorist had just been born.

"The first step is to stay away from the police. Accept the official version of events that your mother was randomly gunned down by a transient. Bury your mother and go about your business. You know nothing. Your mother told you nothing, and they have no reason to fear you." Gray plunged a straw into one of the soda cups. "Can you do that?"

"They have to pay for what they did to my mother, to me. I want them to pay."

"Don't worry, kid. They have a lot to pay for, and we're gonna make sure they do."

Once he started eating, Russell couldn't stop. He finished all three burgers, all the fries, downed a couple of cups of water and then got a soda for the road.

She and Gray saw him into a taxi. As he ducked in, Jerrica put her lips close to his ear. "Olaf will pay for all your mother's funeral expenses and the rest of your education at Columbia. Don't worry about that."

Russell didn't have time to respond, as Gray slammed the door of the taxi.

He shoved his hands in his pockets and spit at the ground. "Poison. They were slowly murdering her kid to make her do their bidding."

"And their bidding was to find *me*, so they know Kiera and Cedar don't know anything about the government database."

"Cedar *does* know something, though. He knows something about Olaf."

"I don't know why he left me that message. Am I supposed to figure out what it means? It's Olaf. So, what?"

"Think about it." Gray bumped her shoulder as they merged with the pedestrians on the sidewalk. "Cedar left that message right after Kiera was shot and an attempt was made to either abduct or kill you. It's Olaf."

A chill zigzagged down Jerrica's back and she

tripped over a crack in the sidewalk. "You mean, as in, it's Olaf who had Kiera killed? No way."

"I know you worship the man, but why not? He's always been anti-government, and the people who are plotting this attack and framing Denver are nothing if not anti-government."

"I don't worship Olaf." Jerrica pursed her lips. "And I know he's anti-government, but that doesn't mean he's willing to kill innocent Americans to make the government look bad. He wouldn't do that."

"It might explain why nobody has orders to kill you. Olaf still has a soft spot for you and while he wants to stop what you're investigating, he's not willing to kill you to do it."

Jerrica punched Gray's shoulder. "Just stop. You have a distorted image of my relationship with Olaf—and you always have. He's almost twice my age for one thing."

"There's about a twenty-year age difference between you. People have those relationships all the time. It's not unusual."

She stopped, turned to face him and grabbed both of his sleeves. "Do you really think Olaf and I are lovers or even want to be?"

"Maybe not on your side. On your side it's more hero worship, but why wouldn't he be in love with you?"

"I can think of a million reasons why. For one,

I'm not particularly lovable." She shook him. "You've given me several more reasons."

"That's because I'm an ass. We already established that." He kissed her right there on the sidewalk. "You're lovable in so many ways, I don't have enough fingers and toes to count them."

Leaning into him, she wrapped her arms around his waist and rested her head on his chest. "I'm glad you're on my side...but you're wrong about Olaf. He loves himself."

He propped his chin on top of her head. "We're impeding traffic. Are we going to walk all the way back to your place or are we going to grab a taxi?"

"Subway stop's right ahead."

As they swayed on the subway in unison, Jerrica tucked a hand into Gray's pocket. "I'm glad Kelly got out of the city. If these people are willing to poison Kiera's son, they wouldn't hesitate to do the same to Amit's girlfriend. I'm lucky. I don't have anyone close to me they can threaten."

"You have me." He kissed the curve of her ear.

She curled her fingers in his pocket. "I'm not worried about you. You can take care of yourself."

"I wish I could say the same about you."

"What do you mean?" She tipped her head back. "I can take care of myself. You know that."

"You're street savvy. I'll give you that." He tugged on a lock of her hair sticking out of the bottom of the cap. "And you know how to take security measures…usually…but these people are different. They're not government, or if they are, they're not playing by any rules."

She snorted softly. "When did the government ever play by any rules?"

"Okay, you have a right to say that." His hand crept to the back of her neck. "When do you think you'll have a handle on the program that can decode the transmissions?"

"I am a super hacker, but I'm not that good. It's going to take a little time. In the meantime, maybe we lure these government moles out of their hiding places."

The train slowed to a stop and rocked back and forth, throwing them together.

Gray put his hands on her waist. "You're going to use yourself as bait?"

"That's the point of going to DC to visit your very well-connected family, right? Memorial Day barbecue to rub elbows with the movers and shakers on the Hill. You know they'll all be there if the Prescotts call. We also know whoever is at the crux of this scheme is a mover and shaker. Has to be."

"You're right." He drilled a knuckle into her back to propel her off the subway. "I'll start setting that plan in motion."

They sneaked into her building through the

alley, and Gray brushed his fist against the chalk dust left by Cedar's message. "I wonder where he went?"

"I wonder *why* he went? He must be afraid of something."

"It's Olaf."

"That makes no sense at all." Jerrica pressed her lips together as she charged up the stairs ahead of Gray.

There was another reason Olaf wouldn't betray her, but she couldn't reveal that to Gray...yet. If they were going to get back together, she'd have to tell him at some point. Or would she? That family of his.

She held her breath as they entered her apartment until she saw Amit asleep on the sofa, the blanket across his chest rising and falling with every breath. This feeling of worrying about someone besides herself was alien.

She'd never worried about Gray, even when he was deployed. The man was solid, impenetrable. She couldn't imagine anything or anyone getting the better of Gray Prescott.

But someone like Amit? She'd never worried about him before, but having him here in her place, dependent on her to help him, caused a whole different strain of feelings in her breast.

She hadn't decided yet whether or not she liked it.

She put her finger to her lips. "Shh. He's out."

Gray picked up a pill bottle and shook it. "Looks like he took a little something for the pain."

"Can you blame him?"

"Not at all, but he's going to have to pull himself together and get out of here. He can join his girlfriend. We can't leave him here alone when we go to DC."

"I know." She pulled the blanket up to Amit's chin. "He's going to lose it when we tell him about Kiera's son and what they did to him."

Folding his arms, Gray leaned against the kitchen counter. "Are you going to check the Cedar message board for anything?"

"I will." Jerrica stifled a yawn. "I don't think he'll use it, though."

"You should set up one of those alerts like you did on the message board you used with Kiera. Then you don't have to keep checking it, right?"

"Yeah. I didn't do it with his because he didn't respond and Kiera did."

"Now we know why she did."

Jerrica rubbed her arms and rose from the sofa. "It's been a terrible night. Imagine how Russell felt—to go through that poisoning all for nothing—they killed his mother anyway."

"We're going to put a stop to all of it, including their sarin gas attack."

Jerrica slid her laptop from the coffee table and placed it on the counter. She accessed the TV message board they used for Cedar's communications and she searched for any posts from Cruz, Cedar's user name.

"Nothing." She snapped the laptop closed. "To be continued tomorrow. I'm exhausted."

"I am, too."

Jerrica gathered her computer, phone and chargers and trailed after Gray up the stairs. She wouldn't mind a repeat performance of last night's escapades, but it didn't feel right to have sex after someone had been murdered in front of you.

When would it feel right? How long would it take to get back to normal life? It had taken her years to even feel anything at all after the FBI killed her family.

If she were honest with herself, she'd been numb until she met Gray. He'd touched something inside her because he hadn't been afraid of her or what she had to say. He hadn't been afraid of her feelings and so for the first time she'd allowed them to spill out in all their ugliness. He hadn't flinched—not once.

As Gray brushed his teeth in her bathroom, she settled cross-legged on the bed with her devices. She checked her phone for messages, and then plugged it in to the charger.

She flipped open her laptop and scanned her email. Her finger froze as she rolled across a message from a Guatemalan coffee company. She double-clicked on the message, and the words jumped from the screen.

I'm okay. Are you okay?

Chapter Eleven

Gray swiped the hand towel across his face and stared at himself in the mirror. He wanted to take Jerrica into his arms and comfort her. Kiera's death had shaken her to the core, and Russell's experience had skewered her heart.

His girl needed a shoulder and a secure place to land, but he didn't want her to think he was making a move on her after the stressful and upsetting day she'd had. That didn't feel right.

As he walked into the bedroom, Jerrica slammed down the lid of her laptop and pushed it onto the nightstand, knocking her phone to the floor. She leaned over the edge of the bed, trailing a hand across the throw rug.

"It went under the bed. I'll get it." He strode across the room on his bare feet, crouched down and retrieved the phone.

"Thanks." She snatched it from him and placed it on top of her computer. Then she sank under the covers, pulling a pillow beneath her head, her face flushed.

Gray cocked his head, shrugged and circled around to his side of the bed. He clicked off the overhead light and crawled between the sheets. "Any news from Cedar or anyone else?"

Jerrica's body stiffened. "No."

"Are you all right?" He placed a hand on her shoulder.

She rolled away from his touch. "What do you think? Kiera's dead. Her son is recovering from a poisoning. Cedar's on the run. Amit's lying on my sofa, battered and weak. Nothing's all right."

"I'm here for you, Jerrica." Gray reached out in the darkness, his hand hovering over her hair. "If you need...anything. I'm right here."

"I just need sleep. Good night, Gray."

He snatched back his hand and buried it beneath the covers. He'd handled that all wrong, but then Jerrica was like a feral animal sometimes. One wrong move and she could scratch your eyes out.

She'd been different on the subway home, leaning into him, seeking comfort he was only too willing to give. What had changed?

His gaze slid to the laptop on the bedside table, just visible over Jerrica's slim outline in the bed. She'd been on her computer when he came out of the bathroom. Had she gotten more bad news?

If so, why would she keep it from him? They were in this together. But then, the woman had kept secrets from him in the past. She'd been raised on secrets and lies…and leopards didn't change their spots.

Not even leopards you loved.

THE FOLLOWING MORNING, Gray woke with a start, sitting upright in the bed, his heart pounding. He reached across the sheets, and he gulped back the panic as his hand swept the smooth emptiness.

When Jerrica's voice floated upstairs, Gray clenched a fist and pressed it against his chest until his heart returned to its normal rhythm. He must've had a bad dream.

He rubbed his eyes and peered at Jerrica's nightstand, now empty of her phone and laptop. He scratched the stubble on his chin. He'd been imagining things last night just because Jerrica had withdrawn from him. He should know her moods by now.

Rolling from the bed, he called downstairs. "Coffee ready?"

"It's alive!" Jerrica called back up to him.

Gray leaned over the railing and peered down at Jerrica's smiling, fresh-scrubbed face. Whatever mood had possessed her last night that led to her shutting him out had passed.

She whistled. "While I sure enjoy the view,

I'm almost certain Amit will not appreciate your nakedness. Put some clothes on and come down here for some coffee. I'd offer you breakfast, but I don't have anything—unless you'd like some oatmeal."

He narrowed his eyes at her long-windedness—almost as if she were trying to distract him from something.

He cleared his throat. "Yeah, about those clothes. They're the same ones I've had on for two days now. I need to drop by my hotel and get my suitcase if I'm going to camp out at your place."

"And you still manage to smell great."

Okay, now she was just buttering him up, and he decided to pop her bubble of effusiveness. "Any news? Get any messages…from anyone?"

"Nope. Cedar is being as elusive as he was yesterday." She wandered out of his view, back into the kitchen.

"And Olaf?" He held his breath and listened for the tiniest exhalation of air or the slightest hitch in her voice.

"Nothing. Nada. Zilch."

He retreated into the bedroom and pulled on his boxers and jeans from yesterday. He sniffed the T-shirt, shook it out and pulled it over his head in resignation.

Heading down the stairs, he almost collided with Amit at the bottom, which would've been a bad thing. The guy could barely walk upright without wincing with each step.

"Whoa." Gray grabbed the bannister and back-tracked up a step. "You feeling better? You're up and about."

Amit tried to raise one shoulder and gave up. "My ribs still hurt like hell, but my head is now just a dull, throbbing mass of pain."

"That sounds…great."

"But I'm determined to get out of here today. I can't stay holed up like a rat clutching a gun in Jerrica's apartment while you two run around and try to save the world."

Jerrica poked her head around the corner, coffee pot in hand. "I told Amit we could get him to Kelly in Boston safely. We can do that, right?"

"Sure." Gray eyed Amit's lanky form as he folded it into a chair at the kitchen table. "But we need to send him off with a decent breakfast. We hardly fed him last night. Man does not live by veggie burger alone."

"Jerrica, I don't know where you got the idea I was vegetarian. Just because I'm Indian?" Amit wrapped his hand around the coffee mug Jerrica had placed before him. "Man, I could use some bacon and sausage."

Jerrica put a hand on her hip. "I'm sticking to my oatmeal, but there's a bodega down the street, on the corner. Maybe Gray could run over there and pick up some groceries for breakfast—if you think it's safe."

"Sure." Gray pulled his socks from inside his boots and sat down. "I can use the alley entrance—and check for more messages."

Jerrica opened a cupboard and stuck her head inside. "You do that, and Amit and I will plot out his escape to Boston."

Gray left the two hackers, heads together over Jerrica's laptop. It looked like they were doing more than making travel plans. He hoped to God they were figuring out a program to decipher the code. They needed answers.

He followed the now-familiar path down to the basement and checked the metal door where Cedar had left his message yesterday. What did Cedar know about Olaf that Jerrica refused to consider?

The sun blinded him as he stepped outside, and he blinked against the light. He made a quick trip to the store and picked up eggs, bacon, potatoes, milk and orange juice, the entire time his head on a swivel.

Had the enemy given up stalking Jerrica's apartment building? They hadn't given up trying to get to her, but an abduction off the street might be too much—even for them. Or would it? The gunman in the park had been willing to whip out a weapon and...do what? Had he intended to shoot to kill, or to snatch her?

Gray bagged his own groceries and headed outside. He stood on the sidewalk for several seconds to assess his surroundings and the people around him. Nobody hesitated. Nobody looked his way.

It was not *him* they wanted, but the bad guys played dirty and they wouldn't be above using him to get to Jerrica, just like they'd used Russell. They'd be barking up the wrong tree on that one—Jerrica wouldn't give up anything to protect him and he wouldn't allow it, even if she wanted to save him.

He ducked into the alley and waited by the door to make sure nobody had followed him. When he returned to the apartment, Jerrica and Amit had good news.

"The translation program just finished. We now have real words in place of the gobbledygook. We just have to figure out what these words mean." She and Amit high-fived.

"You can't write a computer program for that, can you?"

"Not exactly, and we can't turn it over to people who might be able to do it. Hello, I work for Dreadworm. I've been hacking into your computers illegally for years. Can you do some decoding for me now?" She shook her head. "How can we turn this over to someone without getting into trouble?"

"I'll feel out my dad this weekend."

"In the meantime…" She swooped toward him and snatched a bag from his hand. "We'd better get on this—breakfast, I mean. Amit's starving and he has a flight to Boston to catch."

"Is that going to be safe for him? Any ticket purchased in his name might trigger a response from these people."

"Terrorists." Jerrica pulled the eggs from the bag and held them in the air. "These are terrorists, Gray, whether or not they're members of the government."

"You're right. Even more reason to be concerned about Amit's safety."

Amit waved his hand. "I have my alternate ID at the Dreadworm office. I kept it there because I never believed I'd need it."

"Alternate ID?" Gray joined Jerrica in her small kitchen and asked for a skillet.

Amit wedged his hip against the sofa. "Olaf insisted. We all have fake IDs in different names— driver's licenses, social security cards, even birth certificates. We can get bank accounts, credit cards, passports and airline tickets. Luckily I remembered my fake name, and we booked a flight to Boston for my alter ego."

Jerrica opened the package of bacon and

handed it to Gray. "Now we just have to go to Dreadworm and pick up his ID."

Gray asked Jerrica, "You have one of those alternate IDs, too?"

"Of course. Haven't used it yet."

"Hope you never have to."

Jerrica packed a small bag for Amit with a few essentials to take on the plane, so he wouldn't be traveling and arriving in Boston empty-handed. They sneaked him out the back way and traveled a few blocks before ordering a car from Jerrica's phone.

Gray insisted on stopping by his hotel so he could pick up some clothes of his own, and he ended up stuffing a few of his shirts into Amit's bag.

When they reached the general neighborhood of the Dreadworm office, Jerrica ordered the driver to pull over. The three of them navigated their way to the office in broad daylight, and the lack of a tail worried Gray almost as much as having to lose one.

Jerrica flashed her card at the card reader and waited for the click.

Gray opened the door and hustled Jerrica and Amit into the small area at the bottom of the stairs. He pulled the door shut and kept an eye on the video of the alley.

"Me first." He tugged on Jerrica's shirttail and

squeezed past her and Amit on the staircase. He didn't need the jacket today, but he'd worn it to stash his weapon in the pocket. He traced the gun's comforting outline of smooth wood inlaid in cold, hard metal and clumped up the rest of the steps.

If someone were waiting for them they would've come out with guns blazing long before now, so no need for stealth. But he still felt the desire to stand between Jerrica and the unexpected.

As Gray reached the office floor, the whirring and buzzing of the computers greeted him. Then his heart slammed against his ribcage, and he jerked the gun from his pocket.

"Stay right where you are. Make a move and you're dead."

Chapter Twelve

Jerrica drew in a breath and almost plowed into Gray's back. She dropped to a crouch and put her hand behind her to grab Amit's ankle.

The wheels on one of the chairs squeaked as it spun around, and then a smooth, low voice drilled through the hum of the computers. "Don't shoot. I own the place."

Jerrica dropped to her knees in relief and peeked out from behind Gray's broad frame. She choked. "Olaf."

Gray's back stiffened. He stepped to the side but didn't lower his weapon. "This is the world-famous Olaf?"

Amit stamped his feet behind her. "My God. I almost tumbled backward down the stairs."

"You don't need any more injuries, my boy. Come in and rest your bones." Olaf flicked the end of his long scarf at Gray. "You can put the gun away."

Gray shoved the gun back in his jacket, but Jerrica could see his hand in his pocket still holding it.

She scrambled to her feet and crossed the room in three long strides, hitching her purse over her shoulder. Olaf stood to greet her, wrapping her in a bear hug, the scent of his favorite tobacco engulfing her.

"What are you doing here? Is it safe for you?"

"Apparently, it's not safe for you." He pinched her shoulders and set her away from him as his eyes narrowed. "You're traveling with an armed body guard now?"

Turning, Jerrica reached out a hand to Gray. "I'm sorry. This is Gray Prescott. Gray, this is Olaf, Dreadworm's founder."

Gray's jaw visibly tensed, and for a few seconds Jerrica feared the two men would have a standoff, neither approaching the other.

Gray's gaze flicked toward her, and then he made the first move. He approached Olaf as if staking out a poisonous snake, but he held out his hand, the one that had previously been fondling his gun.

"Aren't you supposed to be in hiding?"

Olaf's icy blue eyes crinkled at the corners, but his lips tightened briefly. "I had to come back to rescue my empire, it would seem. One of my New York team dead, one on the run, one beaten and one…stalked."

"Not much of an empire." Gray gave Olaf's hand one last squeeze before he released it, almost tossing it away.

"Ah, you're the Delta Force boyfriend—the one who left Jerrica in the lurch."

Jerrica forced a laugh from her throat. "That's ridiculous. I wasn't in any lurch, and Gray has been our savior these past few days."

"I'll second that." Amit hobbled past the three of them and sank into a chair. "In fact, we just came to the office so I could pick up my fake ID."

"Heading out of town, Amit?" Olaf wrapped his scarf around one hand.

He always had liked to dress dramatically, but Jerrica couldn't help feeling his flamboyance was inappropriate right now. Although technically no longer hiding outside of the country, he still needed to hide.

Jerrica stepped between Amit and Olaf. "Amit is on his way out, but even we don't know where. I figure it's best if we all just keep ourselves to ourselves right now."

Gray had made a sharp move behind her, and she ducked toward Amit's desk drawer to avoid Gray's stare drilling the back of her head.

Amit coughed and grabbed his ribs. "Yeah, totally incognito. Isn't that what you always taught us? I don't plan to show anyone my ID, either, except at the airport."

"Which is where?" Jerrica tugged on the locked drawer.

"It's not in there." Amit struggled to his feet and crossed to the bathroom in the corner. "Give me a little credit. I'm not that obvious. I had instructions to keep it in a secret location, and that's exactly what I did."

Amit emerged from the bathroom with nothing in his hands. Wherever he'd stashed his ID, he now had it concealed on his person. He'd picked up on her direction quickly. She'd never realized how completely she could count on Amit—and now he was leaving.

Amit clapped Olaf on the shoulder. "It's good to see you again, Olaf, but I have to run. I'm a programmer, a hacker. I'm not cut out for danger. I can work on…other things while I'm away. I'll leave the super-secret stuff to Jerrica."

"Where are you staying, Olaf?" Jerrica slipped one strap of her backpack over her shoulder.

"In the spirit of secrecy, I'm going to keep that to myself…for now. Just know I'm safe, and I'll help you as much as I can with this current situation." His light-colored eyes, which gave him an otherworldly look, shifted briefly to Gray. "Can you tell me any more about what you've found in that database?"

The air in the room stilled and if a paperclip

had dropped to the floor right then, it would have sounded like a lead weight.

Jerrica shook her head. "Nothing yet, but someone out there thinks we're onto something—and it must be pretty important."

"Deadly important. It's the database itself and the fact that you breached it…good work." Olaf aimed a tight smile at Gray. "At least some of us think this is good work."

Gray finally moved after holding himself in a tense bundle ever since entering the room. "We have to get Amit to the airport."

"We do, Olaf." Jerrica leaned in and kissed his cheek. "I'm glad you're here, but you'll have to tell me later why and how. If the Feds get wind of your presence, they'll pick you up in a flash."

"They aren't going to get wind of anything. You're the only ones who know I'm here, the only ones who have seen me without my disguise." He squeezed her hand. "We'll talk later and catch up…on everything. Regular channels, my dear."

"Got it." Jerrica took Amit's arm. "Be careful, Olaf. You have no idea what we've been dealing with here."

Gray dipped his head once in Olaf's direction. "Don't do anything to put Jerrica in further danger."

"Seems like you've done a fine job of that already, Lieutenant Prescott."

Clenching his fists at his side, Gray took a step toward Olaf.

Amit put a hand on Gray's chest. "Are you going to help me get out of this city or what?"

Jerrica swallowed. "Let's go."

The three of them left the Dreadworm office in silence, and walked a few blocks before Jerrica ordered a car to take them to the airport.

As Gray stood on the curb, he folded his arms and hunched his shoulders. "So, that's Olaf. Why didn't you tell him everything? Why didn't you tell him Amit was going to Boston?"

"I'm not sure." Jerrica swung her foot off the curb and tapped the heel of her boot against it on the back swing.

Gray lifted one eyebrow. "You finally believe me about Cedar's message?"

"I don't know. It didn't feel right to tell Olaf everything." She poked Amit's arm. "I'm glad you didn't reveal your ID to him…or us."

Amit replied. "I agree. Something doesn't feel right. Why is he here? He knows if he steps foot in this country, he's subject to immediate arrest."

"Maybe what you two are onto is too big for him to pass up. Maybe he wants the credit himself." Gray nudged her shoulder. "Is that the car?"

"It is." She picked up Amit's bag and handed it to him. "That doesn't make sense, Gray. No one hacker gets credit for a data breach. It's all Dreadworm. We're all Dreadworm."

Gray waved at the oncoming sedan. "And right now, that's not a good thing to be."

THEY SAW AMIT safely to the airport and returned to her apartment. As they went through the basement door, Jerrica shook her head at the remnants of chalk dust.

"I don't think Cedar is coming back, but if he never planned to follow up, I wish he hadn't left such a cryptic message." She hooked her thumbs in the front pockets of her jeans, feigning a nonchalance she didn't exactly feel.

With the door closed behind them, Gray turned to her in the stairwell. "Do you really think it was cryptic? Something about Cedar's message must've rung a bell with you. You weren't exactly forthcoming with Olaf when you saw him at Dreadworm...or that surprised to see him."

She flattened a hand against her chest. "I didn't know he was coming back, if that's what you mean, and something about that message *did* make me uneasy. *It's Olaf.* What else could it mean except that he's involved somehow?"

After they entered her apartment, Gray pulled his suitcase toward the stairs. "I'm going to shower and put on some clean clothes. I'm sick of this shirt."

"I kinda like it." She looked him up and down. "Now that we have everything translated, I'm going to take a crack at the code, or at least see if there's some kind of program I can write to decipher it."

As Gray trudged up the stairs with his suitcase in tow, Jerrica released a long sigh. The tension between him and Olaf had set her on edge, but had Gray acted any differently toward Olaf her boss might have been more suspicious than usual.

Olaf knew Gray's family background, knew Gray held him and Dreadworm in low esteem. Olaf hadn't seemed surprised to see Gray at her side, although neither she nor Amit had revealed to Olaf the nature of the data they'd uncovered. As far as Olaf knew, she and Amit had stumbled onto a dark database linked to the government's information banks, suggesting a government employee had access to set something up on the sly. They hadn't told Olaf about Major Denver or even about the terrorist plot.

Now she was keeping secrets from both Olaf and Gray.

She swept her laptop from the counter and settled on the sofa, tucking one leg beneath her and balancing the computer on her knee. She studied the messages back and forth, discussions of mundane office work but obviously filled with code words—words that stood for something else—

much like the codes Dreadworm used on the TV message boards.

Their codes on the fan sites had been predetermined between them on the phone—no way to track down any key. Had these people done the same? Most likely. They wouldn't want to leave a blueprint to deciphering their communications.

"That feels better." Gray jumped from the last step, spreading his arms. "You can come in for a hug now that I'm not wearing the same shirt."

She lifted her laptop. "Love to, but I'm otherwise engaged."

He sat beside her and flicked a strand of hair from her neck. "Are you going to be ready to head to my parents' place in DC?"

"You contacted them?"

"I did. I figured if we're going to stop this thing, we need to be closer to the halls of power."

"Are you going to tell your father what we know so far? It would be good to get someone in government on our side, someone who could make discreet inquiries in the right quarters, someone who can help decode what we have."

"Once we do turn it over, you'll be safe."

"Unless I'm arrested."

Rubbing a circle on her back, he said, "I'm not going to let that happen. I'd like to tell my father what we know without telling him how we know it."

She drummed her fingertips on her chest. "You can blame it all on me."

"I'm not going to do that." He ran a knuckle along the edge of her collarbone. "I want to introduce you to them as my girlfriend, not a Dreadworm hacker."

A little thrill ran down her back. "Are you sure? You told them about me before, and they were not encouraging. I guess they don't want Jimmy James as an in-law."

"They weren't encouraging because they hadn't met you. And your father died almost ten years ago." He caressed the indentation on her throat with his thumb.

She swallowed. "You have to be sure, Gray. I don't want you thinking this is some sexy adventure where we'll catch the bad guys together and then, when we go back to our regular lives, you're stuck with the hacker girl."

"But I love the hacker girl." He cupped her face with the palm of his hand. "I don't think I can live without the hacker girl. Tried it—didn't like it."

Her nose tingled and the words on the screen blurred in front of her. "What if your family hates me?"

"Impossible."

"'Cuz I'm not changing to gain their approval." She swiped her hand beneath her nose.

"Do I look like the kind of guy who needs parental approval for my dates?" He squared his shoulders and puffed out his chest.

"So, you're bringing me home to, what? Prove to your parents that you won't toe the line?"

He grunted, snatched the laptop from her leg and shoved it onto the coffee table. Then he pulled her into his lap, forcing her to straddle him. He took her face in his hands and kissed her so thoroughly, all thoughts of code, Olaf, her father and his parents fled to the hazy corners of her mind.

When she came up for air, she traced the line of his jaw with her finger. "You look like the kind of guy who would protect me at all costs and damn the torpedoes."

"And don't you forget that—ever. I'm never going to let you down again, Jerrica."

Her cheeks caught fire, and she shifted off his lap and scooped up the computer. "I just started working on inputting similar words in this program—names, places, numbers. I think I can get somewhere with this."

He tilted his head, and she could feel his eyes boring into the side of her face. Would he feel so protective of her if he knew the truth about her father?

She had to come clean. He'd just told her he loved her, and she couldn't say it back even though she wanted to...and did with all her heart.

She had to break this code and save Major

Denver for him. Then maybe nothing she had to confess would change his mind about her. He'd be so indebted to her, he'd forgive her anything.

"If anyone can do it, you can." His hand skimmed down her back. "While you're working on that, I'll see about getting my parents' private jet up here to take us down to DC."

"Really?" Her fingers paused over the keyboard. "Do you think it's necessary? Amit flew under his fake ID because he didn't have his own personal bodyguard. As long as you're with me, I think I'll be okay."

"You weren't okay in that alley behind the coffeehouse. You weren't okay in the park. Besides, it's easier this way, and my parents will insist when they realize I'm bringing my girlfriend home." He shrugged. "They like to show off, and they'll want to make a good impression on you."

"Even Jimmy James' daughter?" She wrinkled her nose. "Make sure they know I have beaucoup bucks of my own, and that I'm not interested in you for your money."

"Already told them all about your multi-million-dollar settlement from the government when we were together before. Believe me, the minute I mentioned your name my father probably had a background check done on you."

"That's exactly the kind of thing Dreadworm

fights against—government intrusion into our lives." She ground her back teeth.

"I know. I don't care if you and my parents agree on anything, just that you don't kill each other." He kissed the side of her head. "I'm going to work on our transportation, and then we should think about dinner."

Gray left her to her own tortured thoughts and the repetitive work of scanning the coded messages, finding similar words and plucking them from the text—a perfect complement to those tortured thoughts.

She jumped when Gray placed a hand on her shoulder. "Sorry, hacker girl. Did I scare you?"

"Can you blame me for being on edge?"

His fingers dug into her flesh briefly. "Is that what it is? Stress? You're up and down, back and forth."

"I'm all right." She toyed with his fingers resting on her shoulder. "I couldn't do this without you here, Gray."

"I couldn't do this—" he flicked his fingers at her computer screen "—without you. And I can't do any of it without food. Let's go out and get something to eat."

"Do you think it's safe?" She slid her laptop onto the sofa cushion and stretched her arms above her head, reaching for the ceiling.

"They haven't been able to track us out of this

apartment yet. I don't know if they gave up…or they're planning something else. Does Olaf know where you live?"

"Yes, he does."

"Did Kiera?"

"No." She craned her head around to look at his face. "What are you getting at?"

"These people located you before Amit showed up on your doorstep. They were squeezing info out of Kiera, but they couldn't have gotten your address out of her because she didn't know it. They didn't get it from Cedar."

"How do you know they didn't get it from Cedar? Maybe they followed him here." She rubbed the edge of the tattoo that snaked onto her wrist.

"If they'd done that, they would've been waiting for us in that alley a long time ago. So, where'd they get your address?"

"Maybe it *is* Olaf." She raked a hand through her hair. "But we're back to the motive. Why would Olaf betray the people in his own organization? This type of database, it's Dreadworm's lifeblood. I don't know why he'd jeopardize it."

"Is it Dreadworm's lifeblood? What you and Amit are working on will blow the cover off a covert operation. Covert. This is not government-sanctioned. Dreadworm likes to stick it to the Feds."

"Is that what you believe?" She chewed on her bottom lip. No wonder Dreadworm was a sore spot for Gray.

"Of course it's what I believe." He swept an arm through the air. "You have blinders on, Jerrica. Olaf has brainwashed you."

A knot twisted in her gut. "That's ridiculous. You know why I don't trust the government."

"I do, and I understand that, but what we're dealing with now has nothing to do with the government. It's anti-government. These are rogue operatives within the government, using their positions of power to cause chaos, disrupt our foreign policy, perhaps forge alliances with our enemies."

"I don't want that, Gray. I really, really don't." She yanked on the sleeve of his shirt. "You don't believe that of me, do you?"

"No. I just don't want you to trust Olaf—and it's not because I'm jealous of the influence he has over you."

"Influence." She swept her tongue across her bottom lip. "It's not influence. H-he's my boss."

He held up his hands in surrender. "Okay. Whatever you say. Let's eat."

With Amit gone, Jerrica secured her laptop beneath the floorboards in the spare room and grabbed her purse from the back of a chair. "I'm not sure we need jackets. It's starting to warm up."

Gray stuffed his arms into his and patted a pocket. "I'd wear it if it were a hundred degrees out there. Easier to carry my weapon."

She led the way down to the basement, and they slipped into the alley. This time, they shot across the alley and ducked between two buildings to make their way out to a different street. Each time they had used a different route. If someone circled her building around to the back, they'd find an exit door on the side of the building but only the building next to hers had a door to the alley, and nobody would know to watch that door unless he or she knew about the connection between the two buildings.

This time they exited onto the street next to a dry cleaner.

"Someplace nearby?" Gray took her hand, lacing his fingers with hers as he glanced over his shoulder.

"There's a Mediterranean place about three blocks down. Sound okay?"

"As long as I can get some meat." They walked for a couple of minutes, then he steered her close to a building to get out of the stream of pedestrian traffic and leaned over to tie his shoe…which was already tied.

"What do you see?" She pressed her shoulders against the brick wall, her knees suddenly weak.

"A guy who's been behind us for a block—meandering but always following our path. He just ducked into a shop."

"What does he look like?" Jerrica slid her gaze to the left without moving her head.

"Medium height, baseball cap, jeans, Chucks."

As Gray straightened to his full height, Jerrica pushed off the wall. "What kind of baseball cap? What team?"

Gray jerked his head to the side. "I can't tell from this distance—dark color, blue maybe. Why?"

"Cedar's signature is a Dodgers baseball cap."

"He might be following us to talk to us…or kill us." Gray took her arm and steered her through the crowd.

"That wouldn't be easy if we're in a crowded restaurant." She bumped his shoulder. "Besides, if he's warning me about Olaf, I don't think Cedar is working with him."

"And if it's not Cedar, someone else is following us." Gray brushed some imaginary debris from his shoulder and twisted his head, peering behind them. "Dodgers."

"It's Cedar. Too much of a coincidence." Jerrica wiped her sweaty palms on the thighs of her black pants. "He's not going to approach us out here, so let's keep walking and leave the ball in his court."

"He'd better not make any suspicious moves— or any *more* suspicious moves—than he has already." Gray released her hand and stuck his own in the pocket of his jacket. "Why doesn't he contact you through the normal channels?"

"He heard what happened to Kiera. He probably thinks someone compromised our mode of communication."

"Someone or Olaf?"

"I guess he'll tell us, won't he?" She tipped her head in Cedar's general direction. "Or he's following us to see if anyone else is following us."

"You're giving me a headache. How much farther is this restaurant?"

"A half a block up and to the right."

They trudged on in silence, Gray throwing discreet glances behind them every few seconds to keep tabs on Cedar. "He's still with us."

"Just as long as nobody else is." She poked his ribs. "You've been so fixated on Cedar, have you been paying attention to the rest of our surroundings? We don't have any other tails, do we?"

"That's why Cedar stuck out. I've been scanning behind us ever since we popped out from between those two buildings. We're still good. Like I said before, maybe they gave up getting to you outside your apartment."

They turned the corner, and Jerrica plucked at Gray's sleeve. "It's up there, on the right, blue awning."

Gray opened the door for her, and she stepped

into the noise. Someone would have to be bold to take a shot at them in here—or try to abduct her. Maybe they could enjoy a meal in peace—at least until Cedar got here.

Would he really point the finger at Olaf? She couldn't believe Olaf would ever hurt her, but she hadn't been hurt. That man in the alley had had ample opportunity to knife her. The guy in Washington Square Park had had a clear shot at her. She'd escaped both times, thanks to Gray. But if Gray hadn't been there, would she be dead right now or secreted away somewhere?

She even had an idea of where. She shivered, and Gray entwined his fingers with hers.

He asked, "Are you all right?"

"Hungry and tired. I'll be fine."

The host showed them to a table near the bar. "Is this okay?"

"Yes." Gray pulled out a chair for her and then took the seat facing the door, his back to the bar.

Jerrica leaned in. "You're watching for Cedar?"

"I wanna see his demeanor when he comes through that door. I wanna see his hands."

She ran her tongue around the inside of her dry mouth. "I hope, for his sake, he doesn't do anything stupid."

"You and me both."

Cedar took his time getting there. She and

Gray got water, tea and pita bread, and had placed their order before Gray's eyes narrowed.

Jerrica swiveled her head to the side and watched Cedar, his Dodgers baseball cap pulled low on his forehead, navigate his way through the tables on his way to the bar. His hands swung freely at his sides, and he never even glanced their way.

"So far, so good." Gray's eye twitched and he took a gulp of water from his glass. "What's his plan?"

"Your guess is as good as mine, but as long as he doesn't pull out a knife, a gun or a needle, I'm good."

"A needle?" Gray's eyebrows shot up to his tousled hair.

"I think that's how they poisoned Russell. How else? He'd been at school all day. Someone bumped into him and did something—needle, skin poison."

"All Cedar has is a beer."

Jerrica glanced up as the bartender placed a mug in front of Cedar, who then crooked his finger at a waitress. Jerrica dropped her gaze to her iced tea, stirring it with her straw.

Her cautious coworker wanted to keep their connection a secret. Who was she to blow his cover?

When their food came, Jerrica pointed her

fork at Gray's lamb kebab. "Let me know what you think."

A waitress approached their table with two beers and tossed down a couple of cocktail napkins. "Compliments of your friend at the bar, but he doesn't want any thanks. That's what he told me to say, anyway."

"Okay, well, thank you, then." Gray curled his fingers around the handle and raised the glass to her before she turned away.

"What does this mean?" Jerrica flicked some foam from the top of the mug.

"The waitress placed an extra napkin on the table, right in front of you." Gray tapped it with his finger. "Take a look at it."

Jerrica pinched the edge of the napkin and turned it over. A black scrawl covered the square. She smoothed her thumb across the paper and read aloud in a low voice. "Be careful. Olaf is back. He must be the one who outed Kiera, all of us. I was being followed."

Jerrica's heart fluttered in her chest, and she gulped in a few breaths. "I'm going to reply."

"Go ahead. He's still at the bar."

Jerrica dipped her hand into her purse, pulled out a pen and put the point to the napkin. It scratched the paper. She shook the pen. "No ink."

She dropped the pen on the table and dug through her purse for another. "This one works. What should I write?"

"Ask him how he knows it's Olaf and why?"

Jerrica scribbled the questions on the napkin and asked their waiter to send over the cocktail waitress.

When the waitress arrived, Jerrica crumpled the napkin in her hand. "Can you please take this back to the bar?"

The waitress rolled her eyes, but she took the napkin from Jerrica and walked back to the bar with her empty tray. She dropped the balled-up paper in front of Cedar and returned to work.

Jerrica tried to concentrate on her food, but her stomach churned. Why would Olaf betray them? It didn't make sense. Had these people bought him off, or had Dreadworm always put their interests first? The thought sickened her even more. She pressed a hand against her belly.

"What's wrong?" Gray shoved a water glass toward her. "You look green."

"I don't feel well." She scooted her chair away from the table. "Watch for Cedar's reply. I'm going to the ladies' room."

Gray stood up when she did, his gaze scanning the room.

"It's okay." She patted his arm. "We know we weren't followed—except by Cedar. I'm just humoring him because I know what it's like to be in a state of paranoia."

She threaded her way through the tables to the hallway to the left of the bar. When she reached the restroom, she went into one of the stalls. At the table, she'd felt nauseous, but getting up and moving had helped. As she ripped off a short length of toilet paper to blow her nose, someone entered the bathroom and she leaned to the side to peer beneath the stall door.

A pair of sensible low-heeled shoes planted themselves in front of the vanity, and Jerrica eased out a breath.

She blew her nose and dropped the tissue into the toilet. As she exited the stall, she traded gazes in the mirror with a middle-aged woman washing her hands.

The woman smiled and rinsed her hands while Jerrica pumped the soap dispenser at the sink next to her.

The woman passed behind her on her way to the paper towels, and Jerrica felt a sharp stab in her side.

As she gasped and spun around, she raised her

fist to bash the woman in the face but her limbs turned to warm jelly.

The woman's smile broadened as Jerrica slid to the floor.

Chapter Thirteen

Gray picked up the pen on the table and tapped it against the side of his glass. Maybe Cedar just had a feeling about Olaf and no proof at all. Feelings didn't do them much good.

The pen rattled and Gray wrinkled his brow. He shook the pen again. His pulse ticked up a notch. He pulled the cap from the pen and dragged the point across a napkin, ripping it to shreds.

The blood roared in his ears. He unscrewed the top of the pen and tipped out a black device onto the table. He slammed his fist against the GPS and jumped up.

Out of the corner of his eye, he saw Cedar spin around on the barstool, but Gray didn't have time to explain. He charged toward the restrooms, his heart pounding out of his chest.

Jerrica hadn't been in there long, and he'd seen just one middle-aged woman head into the hallway after her.

Gray slammed his shoulder against the ladies'

room door, but it didn't budge. He banged on the door with his fist. "Open up. Jerrica?"

Cedar drew up behind him and panted. "What's wrong?"

"Someone tracked us here. A pen in Jerrica's purse had a GPS device in it."

Cedar cursed. "I knew it. I knew they'd find a way. I knew Olaf would find a way."

Gray kicked the door with his boot. "Open it now."

A woman's voice answered. "Move out of the way, or she's dead."

"Jerrica?" Gray croaked her name from a throat parched with fear. "I want to hear her speak."

"She can't speak."

Gray dug his fingers into his scalp. "Why not? What did you do to her?"

Cedar touched Gray's shoulder and pointed to a wide-eyed woman at the end of the hallway. He called to her. "Sorry, ma'am. Just a little domestic altercation. My sister got tipsy and locked herself in the bathroom."

"Sh-should I get the manager?"

"Not yet. We'll be out of your way soon."

"Move away from the door." The woman hissed from the bathroom. "Or I swear, I'll end it here."

Cedar pulled at Gray's arm. "Give her space so we can see Jerrica—see that she's okay."

Against every instinct in his body, Gray

stepped away from the door, his muscles aching from tension.

A click resounded from inside the ladies' room and the door eased open. The woman he'd seen earlier wedged her body against the door and pulled Jerrica's limp form in front of her, placing a gun against her temple. "She's just drugged. We won't hurt her. We just need information. That's what she does, anyway, exposes data. We want her to expose it to us."

Cedar growled behind Gray. "Why has Olaf turned on us?"

"Everyone has a price." The woman's lips tightened. "Now move and nobody gets hurt."

Gray took another step back, his fingers curling around a fake inhaler he'd packed earlier.

Jerrica's abductor inched into the hallway, one hand gripping the gun at Jerrica's head, the other arm wrapped around Jerrica's waist to keep her upright.

Jerrica's lashes fluttered, and she formed an O with her lips as if trying to speak. Thank God she was alive—and Gray had to keep her that way.

The woman began to half-drag, half-carry Jerrica in the other direction, to what must be a back exit.

"Wait!" Gray pulled the inhaler from his pocket. "Jerrica has asthma. She's going to need her inhaler if you want her to live through this.

That's what Olaf wants, isn't it? He wants Jerrica to live and if she doesn't, he might stop cooperating with you."

The woman's eyes darted from Cedar, well behind Gray, back to Gray's face. She adjusted Jerrica's body so that it leaned against her own, and then stretched out her left hand. "Put it in my palm. If you grab me or try anything, she's dead."

Gray doubted this woman had authority to shoot to kill, but his hand trembled slightly as he extended his hand holding the fake inhaler. As he leaned in closer, he signaled Cedar behind him to get ready.

The woman ducked her head, and Gray tipped up the inhaler and depressed the button on the bottom of the container, releasing tear gas into the woman's face.

He kept his gaze pinned to the gun in her hand and as she gasped and stumbled back, the gun slipped down from Jerrica's head.

Holding his breath, Gray swung his arm, knocking the gun up to the ceiling.

Cedar dropped to the floor and scrambled toward the woman's legs, throwing himself at her knees.

Her body buckled and she squeezed off a shot.

Panic coursed through Gray's body as Jerrica slumped, but when plaster rained down on them, he grabbed her ragdoll-like form and tossed her over one shoulder.

"We can get out the back. You okay?"

His eyes watering, Cedar choked out some response but he kept low and crawled past the flailing woman, now hugging the wall and gasping for breath.

Gray turned left and ran toward the exit sign down the dark hallway, Jerrica's body bouncing on his shoulder.

Cedar reached the door before he did and shoved it open. Cedar staggered into the alley, gulping breaths of air.

A car idling in the darkness shot forward and squealed from the alley.

"There goes the getaway car." Gray pointed to a dumpster. "Behind here for a minute."

They took refuge behind a dumpster, and Gray thumped a coughing Cedar on the back. "Can you breathe?"

"Barely. How's Jerrica?"

"Conscious but out of it. I don't think the gas affected her that much because she wasn't taking deep breaths to begin with." He thumbed up one of her eyelids. "I can see it affected her eyes, though. We need to get out of here before the police show up. At least the lady had a silencer on her gun, so the shot isn't going to cause immediate panic but someone will discover her soon. I don't know what management is going to make of that scene in the hallway, but I don't want to try to explain it."

"That bitch was no lady." Cedar wiped his own eyes with the hem of his T-shirt. "You can't very well stagger through the Lower East Side with a woman over your shoulder without drawing attention to yourself."

"She can walk. Like you said. She's tipsy. Had a little too much to drink." He pointed to the end of the alley. "Go hail a taxi like only a New Yorker can. I'll get Jerrica in a position to walk her out to the street and the cab."

Cedar took off in a sprint. The kid had guts.

Gray slid Jerrica off his body and patted her face. "Jerrica, can you hear me? Can you walk? You're safe now. I've got you."

She moaned and shook her head.

"I know." He steadied her on her feet. Hanging his arm around her shoulders, he propped her up against his side. "Just move your feet, hacker girl. You got this."

He walked and she stumbled beside him, but she was upright.

When he got to the street, his estimation of Cedar rose again. A taxi waited at the curb, its back door flung open.

Gray poured Jerrica onto the bench seat and

gave the driver the name of his hotel while sliding in after her.

Cedar stepped back from the curb. "I can see she's gonna be okay with you."

"Oh, no you don't." Gray made a grab for Cedar's arm, but the hacker slipped from his grasp. "You're going to tell us everything you know."

"I don't know anything but what I already told you." Cedar put his finger to his lips. "Find out who brought Olaf in from the cold and you'll have your culprit. I do better on my own."

Cedar plucked the baseball cap from his head, shook out his long hair and flipped up the hood of his sweatshirt, melting into the crowd.

The driver barked, "Are you done, man?"

"Yeah, yeah." Gray slammed the door. "Get going."

He kept his eye on the back window, but for all he knew Jerrica might have another GPS planted on her person and whoever Olaf was working with could be tracking them right to his hotel.

He'd have to figure that out later. He needed to get some water into Jerrica, keep her awake. But if she'd been poisoned with the same substance that had been running through Russell's veins, she'd need more than water to come around.

The driver pulled up in front of the hotel and met Gray's eyes in the rearview mirror. "She okay? This ain't one of those roofie things, is it?"

"My girlfriend can't hold her booze. She'll be okay." Gray almost tipped the guy extra, but figured that might look too much like hush money. He added twenty percent to the fare and left it at that.

As he stood Jerrica up on the sidewalk, he whispered in her ear. "C'mon, love. You can do this. Let's get to my room. It's not far."

Her chin dropped to her chest and his heart sank, but then she lifted her head and he could've sworn her spine straightened.

As they walked into the hotel, her head lolled against his shoulder but she kept her body erect and stumbled only once or twice. When they got into the elevator, she slumped against him as her knees buckled.

"You're doing fine. We're almost there."

The door opened on his floor, and he poked his head into the hallway, looking both ways. The empty hallway beckoned.

When they stepped out of the elevator, Gray swept Jerrica up in his arms and cradled her against his chest as he strode toward his room.

Once inside, he sat her on the edge of the bed. "Don't lie down, Jerrica. Not yet. Don't go to sleep."

She blinked her red eyes at him, and he dove for the credenza where two five-dollar bottles of water waited. He cracked open one bottle and sat beside her on the bed.

"Drink this, all of it, even if you don't want to, even if it makes you feel sick. It won't help if you throw up because I doubt she gave you something to eat or drink, so the poison's not in your stomach. I'm thinking maybe the water can dilute its effectiveness in your blood stream, though."

Whether she understood anything he'd just said, she parted her lips, anyway, and he tipped the bottle into her mouth. Some of the liquid ran out the side of her mouth and down the slender column of her throat, but her Adam's apple bobbed as she gulped down what she could.

When she finished the first bottle, he put her to work on the second. She gulped even more of this one down, gagging a few times.

He smoothed her hair back from her damp brow. "How are you? Can you talk?"

She nodded. "Hard to move."

"Maybe she gave you a super-accelerated muscle relaxer, something to make you compliant and keep you quiet, but not to knock you out." He squeezed her knee. "I knew she wasn't going to shoot you. We surprised her. You weren't in there that long, and she probably figured she had time to drag you out the back door to the car waiting in the alley."

"How?" She dug her fist into one eye where the gas had irritated her.

He jogged into the bathroom and soaked a washcloth with cool water. He squeezed it out, folded it into a square and returned to Jerrica.

"I'm going to hold this against your eye. Is it stinging?"

"Uh-huh. How?"

"It was the pen, Jerrica."

She tilted her head to the side, and he pulled the pieces of the pen, minus the GPS, from his shirt pocket and bobbled them in his palm. "The pen you pulled out first, the one that didn't work, had a GPS device in it. You know who put it there, right? They've never been able to track our whereabouts before—not until we ran into Olaf at Dreadworm. He slipped it into your purse when he gave you that hug. I should've never let him near you."

A tear rolled down her cheek from her other eye, but he couldn't tell if it was from the news of Olaf's betrayal or the tear gas he'd sprayed at her abductor.

She dashed away the tear with the back of her hand. "Must've been. Cedar?"

"He's okay. Took off after we got you into the taxi."

She smoothed her hand across the bedspread. "Your hotel?"

"Yeah. Ironic, isn't it? Just when I moved my clothes to your place, I'm back here." He made a half-turn to the credenza. "Coffee? Do you think coffee would help?"

"I do." She switched the washcloth to the other eye.

He measured out the coffee for a single cup and sat beside Jerrica on the bed while it brewed. "Can you tell me what happened in there? Did she say anything to you?"

"Nothing. Said more in the hallway." She cleared her throat. "Came in after me. Washed her hands. Passed behind me. Jabbed me with a needle."

"Unbelievable. Then she planned to walk you out of there and into the waiting car."

"It's Olaf."

The words from Cedar's chalk message took on a whole new meaning now.

"She told us as much in the hallway. Said he didn't want to hurt you, just wants you to stop doing what you're doing." He toyed with the edge of the bedspread. "You could."

She dropped the washcloth from her eye. "No. Major Denver. The terrorist attack. It's real."

"I could take it from here. I have the decoded transmissions. Maybe I could get my father to turn it over to the CIA for further analysis."

"CIA?" She sniffed. "Could be them. Could be someone there."

"I know." He gathered the bedspread in his fist. "This whole thing would've been unimaginable to me six months ago, until I saw how Denver was being railroaded. Even with proof that the initial emails implicating him were false, the narrative about him working with terrorists continued."

"To you." She closed one eye in what could've been a wink.

"What does that mean?"

"Unimaginable to you—not me."

"I know." He jumped up when the buzzer went off on the coffee pot. He slid the glass cup from the coffee maker and wiped the rim with a napkin. He dumped a few of the little creamers into the dark liquid and stirred it with a stick. It would probably be more effective black, but Jerrica wouldn't touch a cup of coffee without a bunch of cream in it.

He brought it to her and slid to the floor next to the bed. "We're going to have to return to your place and get your laptop. Then I think we'd better leave for my folks' place. Do you think Olaf will try to break in? Does he know where you hide your computer?"

She slurped the coffee. "He'll know that I have a backup. Won't do any good to take what I have in my apartment."

"I'm sorry it's Olaf." He circled her ankle lightly with his fingers. "I know he means... something to you."

"He fed my paranoia for sure." She dropped her lashes. "And..."

He waited. When she didn't continue, he glanced up at her. "How are you doing?"

"I'm feeling more in control of my faculties."

"You're talking better. She gave you just enough to incapacitate you to get you out of that restaurant." He unzipped her boot and pulled it from her foot. "I should've never let you out of my sight."

"We were *both* making fun of Cedar for being so careful." She swirled her coffee. "I think I let my guard down because I was with you. You make me feel safe."

"Yeah, and I failed." He stripped off her sock, and she wiggled her toes at him.

"We had no idea I had a GPS in my purse."

"We should've guessed something like that might happen. We were already suspicious of Olaf. Cedar left that message, and there he was in the Dreadworm office. I should've never let him near you." He removed her second boot and sock. "Do you think he was in there trying to disrupt your and Amit's programs?"

"Probably, but even he can't do that. Even if he takes a hammer to the computer, that program is still running somewhere. He can destroy the hardware, but not the process."

"I'll bet he's cursing all the precautions he put in place when first establishing Dreadworm." Gray rubbed his chin. "What's his endgame? I'm sure he wouldn't mind bringing down the government."

"Maybe. I couldn't tell you." Jerrica swung her feet up onto the bed and crossed her legs. "I knew he was no fan, but to be a party to killing innocent people? I didn't see that one coming. Still can't get my mind around it."

"He had Kiera killed, or at least allowed it to happen."

"Had Amit tortured, poisoned Russell."

"And encouraged and abetted your kidnapping—three times."

"Should I meet with him and find out what he's doing?"

He sprang up from the floor and took her empty coffee cup from her. "Absolutely not. We know what he's doing—working with government insiders and terrorists to plot an attack to undermine this country."

She fell back on the bed, her legs hanging off the edge. "I'm so tired. Do you think it's safe for me to sleep now?"

"Sleep?" He stretched out next to her and

slipped his hand beneath her shirt, flattening it against her belly. "I don't recommend it."

She released a sigh and yanked her shirt over her head. "I suddenly have all my senses back, but I want to make sure touch is still working."

She unbuttoned his jeans, and tucked her hand inside his briefs.

He sucked in a breath. "Can we try taste now?"

He rolled on top of her and kissed her sweet, coffee-flavored mouth. "I don't know about you, but my taste is just fine. Only problem is, it makes me want more and more."

His phone, stashed in his shirt pocket, buzzed, tickling his chest. He plucked it out, intending to toss it on the bedside table…until he saw his father's number.

He held the display in front of Jerrica's face. "I'd better take this. It might be about the plane."

"Go for it. I'm going rinse out my mouth since neither one of us has a toothbrush here." She shimmied out from under him.

Gray answered the phone. "Hey, Dad. I booked the plane for tomorrow. Is there a problem?"

"No problem. I just wanted to let you know that Keith will be piloting tomorrow. Randy got called away unexpectedly. You know Keith?"

"I don't think so. Always flew with Randy."

"Keith's reliable. Good pilot. Navy man."

"I'll take your word for it." Gray grabbed a few

pillows and shoved them up against the headboard, and then sank against them. "I have a question for you."

"Fire away." The clinking of ice carried over the phone, and Gray hoped his old man hadn't had enough drinks to fog his mind.

"What do you know about Olaf from Dreadworm?"

Silence answered him on the other end of the phone. Had he caught his father at the tail end of one too many Scotches?

"Dad?"

"Why are you asking about him now? Did you see something on the news?"

"The news?" Gray sat upright. "Olaf's in the news?"

"Not yet. That was the agreement, anyway. He shouldn't be in the news, but that's just it. You can't trust a guy like that."

"Agreement? What are you talking about, Dad?" Gray raised his eyebrows at Jerrica, who sashayed back into the room wearing a black bra and panties.

Sensing his mood, she yanked a white robe from a hanger in the closet and stuffed her arms into the sleeves as she sat on the edge of the bed.

His father's voice came through the line, roughened by the whiskey. "Why are you asking about Olaf?"

"I heard something about him. I'd rather not say how. You first."

"Dammit. If he went to the press and defaulted on the arrangement, I'll have his ass in federal prison so fast his teeth will rattle in that big head of his."

"Agreements. Arrangements. What the hell is going on?"

"As you already seem to know something and you have top-secret clearance, I suppose I can tell you."

"And I'm your son." Gray rolled his eyes at Jerrica.

"The government made a deal with Olaf to allow him to come out of hiding and back to the US."

Gray's mouth got dry and he ran his tongue over his teeth before answering. "What kind of deal?"

Jerrica bumped his shoulder and he put a finger to his lips. The booze had loosened his father's lips, making him uncharacteristically chatty but if he knew he had an audience besides Gray, he'd clam up.

His father coughed. "He's going to stop hacking government databases and turn over everything he has right now."

"You're kidding." Gray's pulse thumped erratically in his temple, giving him a headache.

"I am not."

With Cedar's words ringing in his ears, Gray jabbed two fingers against the side of his head. "Who approved that, Dad?"

"I did."

Chapter Fourteen

Gray's face drained of color, and he white-knuckled his phone. His blue eyes blazed for a second, kindling in his pale face.

Jerrica grabbed his thigh, digging her nails into the denim of his jeans. She mouthed the word *what*.

He choked out one word. "You?"

His lips tightened as he listened to whatever his father had to say on the other end of the line. "Okay, okay. We'll talk then."

Gray ended the call and sat motionless, cupping the phone between his two hands.

"What is it? What did he say?"

Gray swallowed as if he had a lump lodged in his throat. "Olaf is back in the US courtesy of the US government."

"What?" Jerrica crossed her hands over her heart. "How? Why?"

"He made some deal with the government that he would halt all hacking activities and turn over any active projects. In exchange, I guess, he avoids federal prison."

"Wait." Jerrica pinched the bridge of her nose. "Do you think that's why Olaf is trying to stop me?"

"If that were the case, why wouldn't he just tell you? Ask you all to stop your activities so he could return and avoid prosecution."

"Because he knows we wouldn't do it—even to save him." She rubbed his leg. "But it's more than that, isn't it? You looked kinda sick there for a minute."

He stopped fiddling with his phone and put it down on the nightstand. "It's my father, Jerrica."

"What's your father?"

"He's the one who approved the agreement with Olaf." Gray punched the pillow beside him, leaving a fist-sized indentation. "Cedar and I both agreed that the person responsible for Olaf's return was probably the one behind the scramble to shut down your investigation."

Jerrica's jaw dropped. "Your father? You think Senator Grayson Elliot Prescott the Third is actively working against the US government, setting up Major Rex Denver and plotting a terrorist attack? No way."

A little color washed back into Gray's face. "Why else would he authorize this…clemency for Olaf? He hates the guy."

"Did he give you an explanation?" She reclined against the pillows next to Gray and hooked one leg over his thigh.

"He said we'd discuss it when I got home, which is tomorrow, by the way."

"It could be anything, any reason, Gray. You're jumping to conclusions—to the worst conclusion." She reached over and pinched his chin. "Give your father a chance to explain what happened."

He caught her hand and kissed her fingertips. "If the queen of conspiracy theories is willing to give him a chance, I guess I can, too. What is going on? Do you think Olaf is so desperate to deliver on his promise to the government, he'd go to any measures to stop his own employees from getting to the bottom of these secret communications?"

"Doesn't make sense. Olaf made a deal with the government. You'd think he'd be eager to unearth this plot and hand it to the FBI on a silver platter. What better way to get into their good graces? Instead, he wants to make sure it stays secret…and on track. But—" she held up one finger "—if someone in government, someone responsible for this database wants Olaf to put an end to our nosing around, maybe this person offered him a deal. Come in from the cold with no repercussions but make sure your people back off."

"Then he should've just asked." Gray rolled out of the bed. "He had Kiera killed, Jerrica. There's something very wrong with Olaf, but by tomorrow he's not going to be able to get to you."

Jerrica shrugged out of the hotel robe and crawled into bed to wait for Gray while he rinsed out his mouth.

When he slid into bed next to her, his naked body cool to her touch, she wrapped herself around him and got lost in his kisses.

Little did Gray know, Olaf would always be able to get to her.

THE FOLLOWING MORNING, they couldn't wait to get out of the hotel to make sure nobody had broken into her place. She'd been preparing for her security to be breached for as long as she'd worked for Dreadworm, but she'd never dealt with an enemy that actually had the founder of Dreadworm on its side.

She finally let out a breath after quickly checking her apartment and retrieving her laptop from its hiding place. "Nothing's been disturbed."

"What do you think Olaf's next move will be?" Gray wheeled her packed bag next to his by the front door. "I think we should be prepared for the worst, Jerrica."

"The worst?" She wedged a carry-on bag on

top of her suitcase. "He's not going to kill me, Gray. I think we've established that."

"I'm talking about blackmail."

Jerrica's hand jerked and her bag slipped to the floor. "Blackmail? What do you mean?"

"You work for Dreadworm. What you do is illegal. He just might make that deal to save his skin and keep the data hidden—report you to the authorities."

Her hands shook as she reached for her carry-on. "Let him try. If I'm going to be exposed, anyway, I'll reveal the whole sorry mess. Let the CIA figure it out, and if they do have a mole that's their problem."

"Let's see what my father has to say first." Gray clasped the back of his neck. "God, I hope my father's not involved in this."

"From what you told me about the senator, I doubt it, Gray. Think about it. He knows this whole plot is centered around Denver. Do you really believe he'd do anything to harm Major Denver? Anything that could have ramifications for you and your Delta Force team?"

"You reassuring me about my family is a switch." He kissed her hard on the mouth. "Let's get out of here."

They took a taxi to a commuter airfield near the airport and, like magic, Senator Grayson Prescott's private jet awaited them.

They climbed the stairs to the plane and Gray poked his head inside the cockpit. "Keith? I'm Gray Prescott."

"Mr. Prescott." The pilot plucked off his headset and turned in the small space to shake Gray's hand. "Nice to meet you."

"Call me Gray." He tipped his head to the side. "This is Jerrica. She's traveling with us."

"Your father mentioned two passengers." Keith took Jerrica's hand in his. "Welcome aboard, ma'am."

Jerrica craned her neck over her shoulder to take in the cabin of the plane with its reclining seats, television screens and wet bar. "Wow, this is nice. Not what I expected."

"You two sit back and relax, and I'll have you in DC in no time."

When a woman in slacks and a blouse boarded after them and Gray stood to give her a hug, Jerrica's mouth dropped open. "You're kidding me. We have our own private flight attendant?"

Gray laughed. "My father is accustomed to certain amenities. Jerrica, this is Camille."

Jerrica shook hands with the other woman. "Is this an easy gig?"

"The best." Camille put a finger to her lips. "Don't tell anyone about it. I don't want Senator Prescott to get any ideas about hiring anyone else. Do you want anything before we take off?"

"I hate to be demanding, but I'd like a coffee." Jerrica reached for her seatbelt. "I can get it myself."

"Are you trying to put me out of work?" Camille winked and stashed her bag in one of the cabinets. "Cream, sugar? What about you, Gray?"

"Jerrica will have hers with lots of cream. I'll take mine black and if you have any of those breakfast sandwiches on board, we'll take a couple of those."

"I'll get the coffees, but you'll have to wait until we're in the air for the food. Those are Captain Keith's rules. Captain Keith, you want some coffee?"

Keith gave her a thumbs-up. "Yes, please."

Once they had their coffee, the plane took off. When it steadied and reached its cruising altitude, Camille brought them warm breakfast sandwiches, which Gray had ordered for her without meat.

As she bit into the English muffin, it crunched right before the melted cheese hit her tongue. She closed her eyes. "Mmm, remind me why I don't have a private plane."

"Because you're too stubborn to spend the money sitting in the bank." Gray raised an eyebrow in her direction. "Do you have enough in there to buy and maintain your own jet?"

She licked some cheese off her fingers. "I

have no idea how much this all costs, but probably not."

When she finished her sandwich, Jerrica rested her head against the window and stared at the endless blue. Everything in her life felt far removed up here—all her worries, all her problems.

And she had plenty of them.

They touched down in DC after the hour-long flight, and Gray's father's car and driver met them at the airport.

In the backseat of the car, Jerrica smoothed her hand across the leather cushion and whispered, "Is this all courtesy of the American taxpayer?"

"No." Gray took her hand and drew it into his lap. "My father doesn't mix his private business with his government service, does he, Lawrence?"

The driver tapped the rearview mirror. "No, sir. I believe your father is the last honest man in Washington."

Almost a half hour later, Jerrica ducked her head to get a better view of the palatial house as the car rolled through the front security gates. "I guess honesty does pay."

Gray shrugged, as uncomfortable with his family's wealth as she was with her multi-million-dollar settlement from the government.

When the car came to a stop, Jerrica combed her fingers through her hair and tugged her long sleeve over the tattoo that trailed onto the back of her hand, ending with a blue bird.

Gray squeezed her knee. "You don't have to do anything different, Jerrica. They'll like you just the way you are...or not. Doesn't matter to me."

"I know." She turned her head and kissed the side of his neck. "Big house."

"Yeah." He pushed open the back door before Lawrence could get out and open it for them. He did let Lawrence get their bags out of the trunk, as Gray waved at the man and woman standing on the porch.

Jerrica recognized Senator Prescott from the news—a handsome man going silver at the temples, the erect bearing of a soldier. Gray would look just like him someday.

The trim, stylish woman by Senator Prescott's side couldn't wait. She hustled off the porch and threw her arms around Gray. "It's so good to have you home. Just wish you had come straight here instead of taking a detour to New York."

"I had a good reason for that detour, Mom." He disentangled himself from her arms. "This is Jerrica West. Jerrica, this is my mother, Connie Prescott."

Gray's mom gave her a surprisingly firm handshake for such a delicate-looking woman. "Nice to meet you, Jerrica. Of course, Gray told us about you…before, so it's wonderful that you two reconnected."

As Jerrica returned the older woman's grip, she searched her face for signs of artifice, but the smile on Connie's lightly colored lips reached her sparkling blue eyes. Gray resembled his father without a doubt, but he had his mother's eyes.

"I'm so happy to finally meet you. I hope we're not inconveniencing you by dropping by like this."

Connie waved a hand behind her. "Look at this place. Does it look like it would be an inconvenience to house two more people?"

"Well, no."

"C'mon." Connie linked one arm with Gray's and the other with Jerrica's. "Time to meet the old man and don't worry, his bark's a lot worse than his bite."

As the three of them approached the man on the porch, Jerrica took a breath and dropped her shoulders. How bad could it be?

"Dad." Gray shook his father's hand, gripping him by the shoulder at the same time in a modified version of a hug. "This is Jerrica West."

The senator's eyes had lit up as they rested on his son's face, but the lines at the corners of those eyes deepened as he shifted his gaze to Jerrica.

She swallowed and stiffened her spine. "It's a pleasure to meet you, Senator Prescott."

"You can call me Scotty. Everyone does."

His handshake nearly brought her to her knees, but she gritted her teeth and gave as good as she got.

The corner of Gray's mouth lifted as his gaze darted between her and his father. "What is this, a stare-down? You can let go of Jerrica's hand, Dad."

He did, but he didn't release her from his laser-like focus.

"You know, if my son marries you he's going to have a lot of explaining to do on the campaign trail about your background and your connection to that business in New Mexico."

Connie smacked her husband's arm. "Scotty."

"That business in New Mexico? That was my family."

"Of course it was." Connie put her arm around Jerrica's waist. "Let's go inside and have some lunch, unless you want to go to your room and change."

Connie glanced at the hole in the knee of Jerrica's jeans and the different colored laces of her square-toed black boots. "N-not that you need to."

Jerrica climbed two steps and then turned to Scotty, her nose almost touching his. "And Gray has no intention of going into politics, so there's no need to worry about something that ain't gonna happen."

Scotty inclined his head as a muscle ticked at the corner of his mouth.

Gray threw back his head and laughed. "This is going to be a fun weekend."

Connie leaned her head against Gray's shoulder briefly and in a low voice said, "You have no idea."

Jerrica exchanged a look with Gray over his mother's head, but he just puckered his lips and aimed a kiss in her direction.

At least Gray had her back in this lion's den, but it could only get better after that rocky start… couldn't it?

Lunch turned out to be more informal than she'd expected in this house where she'd already caught sight of a cook, housekeeper and gardener.

Connie bustled around the kitchen pulling dishes out of the fridge and setting out cutting boards heavy with meats and cheeses. She stood back from the table, hands on her hips, surveying the feast. "Don't worry, Jerrica. Gray told us you're a vegetarian, and we have plenty of choices for you. I'm heading that way myself."

No drama marred their lunch, as Scotty peppered Gray with questions about his previous mission and Connie kept Jerrica entertained with a steady stream of anecdotes from her stint living in Manhattan and working in the fashion industry.

At the end of lunch, Scotty leaned over to Gray and whispered something in his ear.

Gray drew back. "You don't have to whisper, Dad. Anything you have to show me, you can show Jerrica—unless you're trying to hide something from Mom."

Connie raised her hands. "Nope. I know everything there is to know and couples shouldn't have secrets from each other, so you'd better bring Jerrica along with you."

Gray's eyebrows slammed over his nose. "Now you really have me going. What the hell are you two talking about?"

Bracing his hands on his knees, Scotty said, "This is more than just a secret, Connie."

"In thirty-three years of marriage, you never kept anything from me, Scotty. If you don't take Jerrica with you, I'll tell her anyway."

"When it comes to stubbornness, you took after your mother." Scotty jabbed a finger toward Connie.

Connie gave a genteel snort that flared the nostrils of her nose. "And when it comes to impatience, he takes after you. He's practically jumping out of his skin now, so you'd better show him…and Jerrica."

All this talk of revealing secrets had Jerrica wiping her damp palms on her jeans, and she followed Gray and his father out of the kitchen with a dry mouth.

Connie stayed behind, and Scotty kept his lips sealed as he led them through the massive great room to a set of French doors leading out to a patio area in full spring bloom.

The heady scent of the flowers almost made her dizzy, and Jerrica grabbed onto Gray's hand for support.

He squeezed her hand and nuzzled her ear. "I have no idea what this is all about, but I think my dad actually likes you despite your parentage. I think he was expecting you to be different."

Jerrica jerked back. "You're kidding."

"Not at all." Gray glanced up as they walked across the pool deck toward a grassy expanse. "Are you taking us to the back house?"

His father grunted in reply but never broke his stride.

"You have another house back here?"

"It's like a little two-bedroom cottage. My sister lived there for a while when she moved back here after college, and various employees have camped out there. Maybe they're giving it to us as a wedding gift and to keep you under their eye."

She jabbed him in the ribs even while her heart raced at his mention of a wedding. She hadn't even said *yes* yet. He hadn't even asked. She'd have to stay out of prison first.

As the little house emerged from a copse of trees, Scotty halted on the stone path that led to it. He dug into his pocket and pulled out a set of keys. He dangled them at Gray. "You can go on alone from here. I'll be at the house if anyone needs anything."

Gray cocked his head and snatched the keys from his father. "This had better be good after this cloak-and-dagger business."

His father pivoted away as only a military man could and marched back across the lawn.

Gray tossed the keys in the air and caught them. "Should we start guessing what's in there?"

"No. The cloak-and-dagger stuff, as you put it, has made me even more anxious."

When they reached the door of the house, Gray tried the handle first and then shoved the key home in the lock. He thrust open the door and took one step over the threshold, shouting, "Come out with your hands up."

The click of a gun safety from behind the door prompted Gray to grab Jerrica and shove her behind him.

A bearded man, long hair brushing his shoulders, leveled a weapon at them as he stepped from behind the door. His dark eyes widened for a second, and the hand with the gun fell to his side.

"Is that an order, soldier?"

Chapter Fifteen

With the adrenaline still pumping through his body, Gray launched himself at his commander and threw his arms around the shoulders that weren't as broad as they had been.

"Rex! Major! I mean, sir."

Denver smacked him on the back a few times. "In the flesh."

"What are you doing here?"

"Probably the same thing you are." Denver shoved him aside. "Are you going to introduce me to the lady? I already know she's the infamous Jerrica West, and she's probably gonna save my life."

"Jerrica—" Gray circled his fingers around Jerrica's wrist and pulled her forward "—this is Major Rex Denver. Major, this is Jerrica West, Dreadworm hacker extraordinaire."

Denver took Jerrica's hand in both of his. "You can call me Rex—you both can, for now. I'm sorry this whole mess has put your life in danger, Jerrica."

"It's not your fault, Rex. Amit, my coworker, and I had already stumbled onto this before Gray showed up and we even had a clue what it all meant. If Gray hadn't come to New York, explained everything and protected us, I'm not sure where we'd all be right now."

"How close are you to figuring out the code?"

"We figured out the first level of the code, thanks to the wheel you sent Gray." Jerrica tapped her index finger against her temple. "But without understanding the secondary code—names, places, and so on—I'm not sure we can get much more out of it. We need to turn it over to someone who can decipher it, but I'm afraid to step forward, afraid to explain how I got the communications in the first place."

"Which is why you're here, right?" Denver raised his brows at Gray. "I'm assuming that's why you came to visit your parents. Having this code is not going to do you much good in Manhattan."

"That explains what we're doing here, but what the hell are *you* doing here? How'd you get into the country?"

"It's a long story and telling it would put too many people at risk, but I had to come in. I had to trust someone—other than you guys. Senator Prescott's on the Armed Services Committee, and, well, he's your dad." Denver studied the gun in his hand before shoving it in the back of his waistband. "I'm surprised nobody went to him before this."

"We didn't know who we could trust, if we could trust the people around him. You know my father—" Gray saluted. "By the book. I didn't even know if he would believe our story about an insider, a mole in our own government."

"I understand, but I think we have enough proof now. Cam was able to expose as fakes the initial emails that pointed to me. Asher figured out he was brainwashed at a government-run medical facility and used to implicate me. Joe put a stop to the lie that I had anything to do with that bombing in Syria. Logan and that young marine's sister were able to verify that something was amiss at the embassy outpost in Nigeria and Hunter was able to ID the terrorist group behind it all." Denver swiped the back of his hand across his nose. "You guys did good. You did more than I expected."

"We weren't going to let it stand, sir… Rex. We weren't going to sit by and allow others to smear your name."

"But it's beyond me, isn't it?" He leveled a finger at Jerrica. "This young lady right here can verify that fact—a terrorist attack on US soil, one that I got word about, one that I had started investigating with my sources in the field. I only had bits and pieces, but you tapped into the whole plan."

"Tapped into it but can't figure it out." Jerrica waved a hand behind her. "Do you think Scotty can help us with the rest?"

"Scotty?" Denver quirked an eyebrow.

"Oh, yeah." Jerrica crossed her fingers. "Me and him are like this."

Denver's laugh rumbled in his chest. "He's a tough nut, but he'll do what's right. He'll always do what's right, like you, Jerrica. Isn't that what Dreadworm's all about? Doing the right thing? Transparency?"

Jerrica's body stiffened beside him, and Gray draped an arm across her shoulders. "It looks like Olaf, Dreadworm's founder, has had a change of heart. He's been setting up his own staff, including Jerrica, to keep them from revealing the transmissions they uncovered."

"Is he working with the terrorists? The government?" Denver clasped both of his hands on the back of his neck. "The terrorists and some members of government are one and the same, aren't they?"

"M-my father was responsible for allowing Olaf back into the country. He already told me that Olaf was offered immunity and free passage back to the US in exchange for calling off Dreadworm, but Jerrica and I know he's working with someone else to keep the transmissions under wraps. One of Jerrica's coworkers at Dreadworm implied that whoever let him back in was the government mole."

Denver tugged on the end of his long beard. "Jerrica's coworker doesn't know much about how government works. Senator Prescott may have given the final order, but he didn't make that decision on his own. Hell, he probably wasn't in favor of the decision. We'll have to ask him what the official reason was for allowing Olaf back in without facing ramifications and who suggested it—that could be our mole."

Denver circled the room once. "What's the plan? You're going to crash your parents' big Memorial Day party with all the movers and shakers?"

"I'm going to be the bait." Jerrica raised her hand. "We think at least one of the government plotters will be in attendance. We think he…or she…will make a move once he sees me and Gray here, figuring that we either turned over the communications or are planning to do so."

"And if they don't make a move? If they play it cool?" Denver swept his hair back from his face and tucked it behind one ear.

"Then we'll make *our* move." Gray clenched his teeth. "One way or the other, this ends this weekend."

BACK AT THE main house in one of the many spare bedrooms, Gray stretched out on the bed. "I'm glad he's back, safe."

"He's not safe yet. Do you think he'll be okay hiding out here?"

"Nobody even knows whether Major Denver is dead or alive. I'm sure nobody suspects he's stashed away at a US senator's house. You heard him—my father even has extra security on the property, which won't look odd considering he's going to be hosting half of the government here in a few days."

"Is it going to be the good half or the bad half?"

"We've made progress for you to admit there *is* a good half." He patted the bed beside him. "You don't need to pace around the room. We're safe here."

Jerrica sank down next to him, but kept her feet firmly on the floor. "If we turn over the transmissions to your father, what's he going to do with them and will I get in trouble for having them?"

"My father wouldn't take any action against you, but it might be out of his hands."

"That's what worries me." She leaned back and rested her head on his stomach. "I need to crack the final piece that leads me to the computer generating the orders, and we need a date, time and location for this attack. I know it's in the reams of data I have. Someone just needs to make sense of it."

Gray massaged her temples. "We're close. It's going to be okay, Jerrica."

"There's still so much I don't understand about Olaf's involvement. He turned on Dreadworm to, what? Get back into the country and avoid prosecution? That doesn't seem like enough of a payoff to me."

"That's why I think it's more than that." He flattened the line between Jerrica's eyes with the pad of his thumb. "I think he's involved in the plot. It's his ultimate way of getting back at the government, the government he's been at war with for years."

"I suppose you're right." She rolled her head to the side to look into his eyes. "Maybe I can get to him. Maybe I can convince him to tell me who he's working with. He can still get his immunity if he starts playing for the other side."

"I don't want you anywhere near him, Jerrica. We don't know what his motives are and even though you had a close relationship with him… once, he seems to have forgotten about that." He brushed the back of his hand across her cheek. "Come on. I'll show you the rest of the house before the hordes descend for the party."

"Hordes of politicians and government officials?" Jerrica rolled from the bed and flipped back her hair. "What could possibly go wrong?"

MEMORIAL DAY DAWNED with sunshine and promise. For the occasion, Jerrica shunned her customary black in favor of a colorful skirt and poppy-red top. A pair of sandals replaced the black boots, and she'd even had a pedicure the day before.

As she stood in front of the full-length mirror in the bathroom, wiggling her red toes, she smoothed the skirt over her thighs. If she had to come out as a Dreadworm hacker and get taken into federal custody, at least she'd try to look innocent.

Gray appeared behind her, wearing a pair of board shorts with the American flag emblazoned across them and a blue T-shirt that matched his eyes. Those eyes met hers in the mirror.

"You look...pretty, but don't think you have to change your style to fit in with these people."

"That's not it. First of all, it's too warm to wrap up in black jeans and boots." She stroked on some mascara and blinked her eyes. "Secondly, if I'm going down, I'm not going to look the outlaw part as they take me away in cuffs."

Gray rubbed her arms. "Nobody is going to take you away in handcuffs."

"Really?" She smacked the tube of mascara down on the vanity to her left. "Because it's time, Gray. I can't make any more progress on the code by myself. We have to turn it over to someone who can, to someone who can stop this terrorist attack, exonerate Major Denver and bring these rogue officials to justice. It's time for me to place my trust in the process."

He turned her around to face him and lightly kissed her lipsticked mouth. "Can you trust me, too? You're almost family. My father's going to do everything in his power to protect you—and as you've pointed out many times before, my father has a lot of power."

She snorted and then dabbed her nose with the tissue crumpled in her hand.

Gray swept her hair from her shoulder and pressed a kiss against her bare skin. "Let's pay another visit to Denver before we wrestle with the snakes at the party."

After a brisk walk, they arrived at the cottage. Denver opened the door before they could knock.

"I saw you coming." He snapped the door closed behind them and locked it, even though private security roamed the grounds. "Any news?"

Jerrica nibbled on her bottom lip. "I'm going to have Gray's dad point me in the direction of the most sympathetic FBI or CIA officer, and I'm going to come clean."

"I thought you'd come to that conclusion." Denver tipped his head toward Gray. "Do you agree?"

"I think Jerrica will be safer in federal custody—if that's the way it goes—than dodging terrorists and government insiders."

"Seems that we'll both have to put our faith in others, Jerrica." Denver dragged his fingers through his long hair. "We're both on the line here."

"You haven't actually done anything wrong, though." She drove a thumb into her chest. "I have."

"I went AWOL, off the grid. That's not allowed for a soldier, no matter what the circumstances." Denver held up a glass of water to the window and peered into it as if looking into a crystal ball.

"What do you see in there?" Gray pinged the glass with his finger.

"Help. Reinforcements." Denver winked. "They're on the way. I can feel it."

"Well, you've been lucky so far." Jerrica squeezed the major's biceps. "I'm gonna stick with you and maybe some of it will rub off on me."

Gray rolled his eyes. "You're talking about Major Denver here. No luck involved. However he survived, however he got here, it had nothing to do with luck and everything to do with training and skill...and maybe a little badassery, and you possess all of those qualities, hacker girl, especially that last one."

"I got here because of you." She fluttered her lashes at him. "Plain and simple."

They all jumped at the knock on the door.

Gray peeked through the blinds. "It's my father."

"Then you'd better let him in. He does own the place." Denver strode past them and threw open the door. "Join the party, Scotty."

The senator's gaze darted to each face. "It's about time someone invited me to this party and told me what the hell is going on under my own roof."

Jerrica squared her shoulders and stepped in front of Gray's father. "I work for Dreadworm, and my coworker and I hacked into a clandestine database connected to the CIA's. We uncovered a plot involving an attack using sarin gas and blaming Major Denver, all engineered by dark forces within the government. We need help deciphering the code to find out the who, the when and the where."

Jerrica held her breath as Scotty took it all in with an unfathomable expression on his face. He finally blew out a breath and said, "It's what we suspected."

Denver and Gray erupted at the same time, talking over each other until Scotty held up one hand. "Not all of it, we didn't know all of it. I didn't know my son's girlfriend worked for

Dreadworm and I didn't know about this database, but we've been receiving communiqués, threats from someone within the government to release certain prisoners, to take certain steps and approve certain agreements with countries that are all in our worst interests."

"Threats?" Gray rested his hands on Jerrica's hips.

He must've sensed she was about to keel over after her outburst.

Scotty dipped his chin to his chest. "Threatened as in, 'do these things or else.'"

"Or else what?" Denver wedged his hip against a table, crossing his arms. "Or else they release the sarin gas?"

"You got it, although we didn't know it was sarin. They threatened the leadership of the CIA, the FBI, the president himself."

"Was Olaf part of that deal?" Gray pinched Jerrica's waist.

"He was. The FBI has been working on several leads to track down who's behind this plan, using information unearthed by your Delta Force team. I know they believed their efforts to clear Major Denver were going nowhere, but we've had to be as secretive as the other guys. We don't know who to trust." Scotty leveled a finger in Jerrica's direction. "But we've never had computer exchanges between these people before."

Jerrica put a hand to her throat. "I have everything on my laptop, and my laptop is here. I-I can turn it over right now, if you want. The sooner the better."

"We'll have to wait until after the party." Scotty jerked a thumb over his shoulder. "The guests have already started arriving, and we don't want to alert anyone."

"I have a feeling Jerrica's presence is going to be an alert to someone. If anyone who's part of the plot attends this shindig, he or she might already know who Jerrica is."

"Let 'em try doing something in my house to my future daughter-in-law." Scotty's eyebrows formed a ferocious V over his nose, causing Jerrica to quake in her sandals and she wasn't even the target.

In fact, Senator Grayson Prescott wanted to protect her—his future daughter-in-law.

"Now let's get out there and play nice, or your mother's going to have my head on one of those silver platters currently displaying hors d'oeuvres too pretty to eat."

Scotty crooked his arm and motioned to Jerrica. She grasped his elbow, and Gray took her arm on the other side and brushed his lips against her ear. "I told you he liked you."

Jerrica floated into the party between the two Graysons. Gray's father hadn't called for her head when she'd made her big announcement. Maybe he could keep her safe—like son, like father.

Connie cut a path through her guests, who were already imbibing mimosas and Bloody Marys and selecting appetizers from the trays artfully deployed across the lawn, making a bee-line for their little group, her fine features alight with fire.

She started speaking before she even reached them, her arms flung out to her sides. "I can't believe he had the nerve."

"Uh-oh." Scotty squeezed Jerrica's arm. "Someone must've brought a lady other than his wife or decided to wear white shoes."

"Can't be that. Memorial Day is when you're finally allowed to wear white shoes—if you really want to." Gray grabbed one of his mother's restless hands but she twisted away.

"You're both so funny." She shook a finger at her husband. "But you're not going to be laughing when I tell you what happened."

A murmur swept through the guests, rising and then falling to a whisper, the sound causing the hair on the back of Jerrica's neck to stand on end.

Scotty pinned his gaze to where the crowd parted and then spluttered. "Is the man out of his mind?"

Jerrica stood on her tiptoes to see the commotion. Her blood, racing through veins, turned ice cold as her eyes met the light blue ones of Olaf.

Chapter Sixteen

Jerrica grabbed Gray's sleeve. "What's he doing here?"

"That's what I want to know." Scotty took a menacing step forward, but Connie placed a restraining hand on his arm. "You can't toss him out on his ear in front of everyone. Assistant Director Collins brought him, along with the press clamoring at our front gate. You can tell him in no uncertain terms that Olaf is not welcome in my home, and I don't appreciate unapproved guests."

Gray made a sharp move and a half turn toward his father. "Collins, the assistant director of the CIA?"

"One and the same." Scotty's eyebrows formed a single line above his nose. "What do you think?"

"What do you think he wants us to think?"

Like a bird's, Connie's head swiveled back and forth, following the conversation between her husband and her son. "I don't know what you two are talking about, but Patrick Collins just brought the most notorious political figure of the day to my Memorial Day party…and I'm not happy."

"Plaster a smile on your face, Connie, and welcome your new guest." Scotty laced his fingers with hers and gave her a tug. "I'll explain everything later."

Jerrica licked her lips as she watched Gray's parents approach Olaf. "What should I do, Gray? Should I pretend I don't know he's behind the disruption at Dreadworm? Should I accuse him? Call him out? Denounce him publicly?"

"Let's play this by ear. Maybe Collins just outed himself as the mole, or maybe he doesn't realize we know about the plan."

"If Olaf told Collins, his good friend and savior, he knows." She tapped a passing waiter on the arm and snagged a mimosa. She downed half the drink and then snatched a couple of crab puffs from another tray and stuffed them into her mouth.

Did Olaf know she'd be at this party? He must've known. By the tilt of his smile when he spotted her, he had something planned—and it wasn't going to be pleasant. She had to find out about it before Gray did.

She patted her lips with a napkin. "Okay, let's hang back and watch what happens."

So many dignitaries crowded the lawn and the

pool deck, half of them wanting to shake Gray's hand and discuss his political future with him, that it didn't take Jerrica long to escape Gray's realm and shimmy up next to Olaf.

She lowered her voice and rasped, "What the hell are you doing here?"

"It's my coming-out party. I'm here legally, and everything is above board. I'm free."

"What price did you pay? Or did someone else pay the price for you? Kiera? Her son? Major Denver?"

Olaf clicked his tongue, as a breathless woman headed their way. "I have so many fans wanting to speak with me, I can't talk right now. Meet me by the front gate in ten minutes. I have a proposition for you—you alone. Don't bring anyone with you, or...well, you know what could happen."

Jerrica's heart slammed against her chest, rattling her ribcage. She knew it. Olaf wasn't done with her yet.

She glanced over her shoulder at two men, their heads together with Gray's. They must be salivating over his potential as a political candidate— young, good-looking, connected, military. They obviously didn't know about the Dreadworm girlfriend who would totally and completely torpedo any chances he had at a career in politics—if he was still with her when he decided to throw his hat in the ring.

She ducked her head and scurried to the kitchen where controlled chaos reigned as the caterers moved in and out in a dance choreographed by Connie's chef.

Jerrica dug her elbows into the center island and buried her chin in her hands to wait out the ten minutes. Her mind raced as fast as the waiters whisking food out to the guests. She had an idea of what Olaf would propose, and her answer would be the one that would keep Gray safe.

Connie's chef gave her a nudge. "You're in the way—go socialize."

Jerrica gave the woman a half smile and slid out the door of the kitchen into the dining room. A few of Connie's guests bunched together, holding conversations in low voices. Gatherings like this must have a lot of hush-hush social interactions—like the one she was about to have.

She traipsed across the great room and out the front door, looking left and right. The Prescotts had created a path from the drop-off point outside the main gate to the side gate leading to the backyard. Most of the guests had already arrived and the parking valets lounged against the cars, smoking cigarettes and checking their phones.

Her sandals crunched the gravel as she made her way outside the gate to the guard shack in front of the property.

Her phone buzzed in the purse strapped across

her body, and she checked the text message from Gray. She ignored his question and tapped the record button on her phone.

She scooped in a deep breath and rounded the corner of the guard shack. The branches on the bushes at the head of a trail that snaked into the woods bobbed and swayed, but nobody stepped forward.

Two seconds later, Olaf materialized on the path, his white-blond hair creating a bright spot in the foliage. How'd he get out here so quickly when she'd left him with an adoring fan?

Folding her arms, she dug her nails into her biceps. "What's this proposal?"

"So abrupt, after all we've been through together." He flicked his fingers at a bug flying in front of his face.

"I could say the same about you. Your attack on Dreadworm was so abrupt after all we've been through together. Or was it? How long have you been a part of this plan?"

"You know I don't reveal much of anything, Jerrica, even to you."

"What do you want from me?"

"It's easy, really. I don't want you to do *something*. I want you to do *nothing*. Do nothing with the information you hacked, so skillfully, I might add. I had assured my…companions that nobody would be able to break into that database I helped them create." He lifted his shoulders. "But I guess I created a monster, didn't I?"

"You helped them devise a means of communicating via computer and helped them with those emails implicating Major Denver."

He raised his hand. "That was I. Who else?"

"Why Major Denver?"

"Wasn't that a nice touch? Although in retrospect it was a mistake. We had to get rid of Denver somehow because he was onto the plan, but his setup was my idea. I thought I would be giving the finger to that Delta Force lieutenant who'd broken your heart. I had no idea he'd come crawling back to you. But then again…"

"What?" Jerrica barked the word so loudly, a startled bird took flight from a tree next to Olaf.

"Did Prescott really come groveling back to your bed because of your…charms? Or did he worm his way back into your affections to help his commanding officer?" Olaf brushed his hands together. "I guess we'll never know, but that doesn't concern me now."

"It's too late."

"What's too late?" Olaf's eyes glittered like chips of glass.

"I already told Senator Prescott about the database. He's going to make arrangements to have someone decode what I couldn't. It's over, Olaf."

"Oh, it's never over, Jerrica. You of all people should know that."

"How about me?" Gray materialized beside her. "*I'm* saying it's over for you. It's only a matter of time before those secret communications are decoded, and your plans to take over the government are finished."

"A matter of time. Yes, time can be our enemy or time can be our very good friend." Olaf placed his hands together and gazed into the distance over his fingertips. "At this moment, we have a drone loaded with a canister of sarin gas. Its destination? This lovely garden party."

"No!" Terror clawed through Jerrica's insides, as Gray reached for her hand. "And you're controlling it?"

"I do have control of it, but it's not operational…yet. We get what we want, that drone stays grounded."

"You people are insane." Gray lunged toward Olaf, but Jerrica grabbed his arm.

"Maybe, but we hold the cards." Olaf crooked his finger at Jerrica. "Come with me, Jerrica, and I'll tell you my proposal."

"She's not going anywhere with you." Gray put his arm around her and drew her close.

This time, she didn't melt into his body. She kept her frame stiff, her mind alert. "Anything you tell me, Gray can hear, too. Besides, you already told me to destroy the database I uncovered and the program I used to uncover it. That's not going to happen—I don't care how many drones you have coming. It's proof, and I'm not going to destroy the proof of who's behind this attack and why."

"Are you sure about that, Jerrica? All of it? I'm not done with my proposal, and I don't think you want your bodyguard, or whatever he is to you, to hear all your dirty little secrets."

A tremble ran through Jerrica's body, but she dug in her heels. "He can hear anything. Spit it out, Olaf. What's your proposal?"

"Destroy your work—it's not too late. You can disable anything you handed over to Senator Prescott, and I will deactivate the drone."

"What else? I know there's more."

Olaf spread his hands. "Or I'll turn in your father."

GRAY JERKED AND took a step back from the words that hung in the air between them. His arm seemed pinned across Jerrica's shoulders, but he shifted to the side to study her profile. "What's he talking about? Your father is dead, killed in the FBI raid on his compound."

"No, he isn't." Jerrica ducked away from his arm, taking a step closer to Olaf. "My father is not dead, Gray. He escaped and made his way to

Guatemala. He's been hiding out there for years…
most recently with Olaf."

Gray curled his hands into fists, not knowing whether to punch Olaf's grinning face or the
wall of the guard shack behind him. "And you've
known this how long? From the beginning?"

"I found out a few years after the raid."

"So, you knew when we were together…the
first time."

"I did. I also planned to tell you this time."

Olaf snapped his fingers. "While I'd love to
stand here and listen to you two work out your
relationship issues, time is of the essence. That's
the deal, Jerrica. You destroy your program, I'll
call off the drone and nobody has to know about
Jimmy James living in hiding—well, except the
lieutenant here, but that's on you now."

Gray held his breath. No way would Jerrica
put the country at risk for a father who'd put his
own family in danger. No way would she put her
relationship with her father over her relationship
with him.

Jerrica puffed out a breath. "Deal."

Olaf crowed as Jerrica's response kicked Gray
in the midsection. He almost doubled over, but
he held himself erect. "You'll pay for this—both
of you."

"Sorry, Gray, but this is my father we're talking
about. I have to protect him against the govern-

ment who harmed him, harmed us, my family."
As she spoke to him, she turned toward him, a
stranger to him now. Or maybe she always had
been.

She blinked her eyes at him rapidly. "I'm going
to leave with Olaf now. He'll help me stop the
program, and he'll stop the drone. Once he and
his forces take over the government, Major Denver will be exonerated. People will know he was
used."

Was she signaling him? Olaf may have gotten
the same idea as he moved forward to watch her.

"But we'll be living in a country held hostage
by lunatics who want to do who knows what? Is
that the country you want?"

She shrugged. "I don't care. This never was my
country after I lost my mother and my brother."

Dragging her phone from her pocket, Jerrica
said, "Olaf, I need assurances from you that my
father is okay. He sent me an email the other
night, so I know he was fine then, but I need to
know that now."

Gray swallowed. She must've heard from her
father the night her mood changed and she returned to her secretiveness.

"Text away. No harm has come to Jimmy. I've
taken good care of him all these years...and you.
Gave you a job you could've only dreamed of."

He flicked one end of his scarf over his shoulder. "And then we get to work on your computer."

Jerrica looked up from her phone, her fingers still moving. "*Your* computer. I turned mine over already, but I can work on the program from yours. You do have your computer with you, right? You never go anywhere without your computer."

"Come on, then." Olaf waved a hand at Gray. "You'd better make sure your protector here knows that if anything happens to me, orders are in place to release the drone, and if he goes running back to his parents' party and tries to evacuate the place, the drone will be activated and if the gas doesn't kill these people, it will be released elsewhere. Do you want that on your conscience, lieutenant?"

"Go! Take her. You two deserve each other but if you think you and the other terrorists are going to stage a coup and run this country through threats, you haven't reckoned on the force of the US military."

"Hollow words, lieutenant, but good luck with that."

As Olaf led Jerrica into the woods and presumably to his computer, she twisted her head over her shoulder one last time and…winked and tipped her head down.

What the hell did that mean? His heart held onto the hope that Jerrica was playing Olaf, but his brain reasoned that she'd lied about her father. She'd lied about Dreadworm when he'd first met her. How many other lies had she told him? Had her body lied to him, too?

And how would she be playing Olaf? She couldn't overpower him physically. Perhaps she'd make a show of dismantling her program when she really had it backed up somewhere, but Olaf and his cronies still had a drone weaponized with sarin. The database implicating all the players wouldn't do them any good with that threat hanging over them.

As he turned to go back to the doomed party, the blood pounding in his eardrums, his eye caught a glinting object in the mulch on the ground. He took two long steps and scooped up Jerrica's phone, the one she'd been using to text her father. Had she received a response from him? She seemed to have forgotten she was waiting for one.

He turned the phone over in his hand and his eyes widened at the sight of a long, unsent text message. Had she forgotten to send it? Was her loyalty so strong for Olaf in the end that not even her father mattered?

Cupping the phone in his palm, he skimmed

the message and then tripped to a stop. The message wasn't meant for her father; it was meant for him.

Chapter Seventeen

Gray rubbed his eyes and brought the phone close to his face.

Give me ten minutes to get onto Olaf's computer. Then evacuate the party. Watch who leaves first. My program holds the key to disabling the drone. Trust me.

He peeled his tongue from the roof of his mouth and ran it across his teeth. *Trust me.* Could he do it after all the lies?

If Jerrica were really playing for Olaf's team now, why would she want him to evacuate the party? Maybe she and Olaf wanted to take the plan to its fruition and stage the coup right now.

Telling everyone to leave the party would be a signal to make the drone operational. Maybe they had it planned so that nobody would be able to get out in time. His parents. Major Denver.

He worked his tense jaw back and forth. Jerrica

had lied about Dreadworm, and she'd lied about her father—but nothing else. She'd been working as hard as he had to get to the bottom of this. She wouldn't throw it all away now.

He thought she'd been a stranger when she talked of joining forces with Olaf and protecting her father, but when she'd turned and winked at him—she was the Jerrica he knew...and loved.

Trust her? Hell, yeah.

Checking Jerrica's phone for the time, Gray strode back to the house, the music floating into the driveway a strange accompaniment to the terror about to be unleashed—sort of like the orchestra playing on the deck of the *Titanic*.

As he charged into the great room, his jaw dropped. Five clean-cut men surrounded Major Denver, bearded and scruffy and smiling. "There he is. Prescott kept Jerrica safe, and she's ready to give us the goods."

His Delta Force teammates started forward and then stopped, the laughter falling from their faces.

Cam Sutton ate up the rest of the space between them and thumped him on the shoulder. "What's wrong, Prescott? We should be celebrating about now."

"Am I glad to see all of you." He glanced at the clock on the phone.

"You don't look it, bro." Hunter Mancini's dark

eyes narrowed. "We were under the impression there was a nuclear attack planned, and your girl unearthed the real plan. I'd say that's a lot to be thankful for."

"Yeah, the real plan—sarin, a canister of it attached to a drone."

"My God." Asher Knight, still looking thin after his captivity, clasped the back of his neck with one hand. "These people are diabolical. Once Jerrica's intel is decoded, we'll know who's behind this?"

"I think we'll know a lot sooner than that." Gray tapped the phone where ten minutes had ticked away since Olaf left with Jerrica. "We have to evacuate this party—now. Keep an eye on the guests who are moving the quickest and most suspiciously."

"Wait." Joe McVie raised his hand. "Is this some kind of ploy to smoke 'em out?"

Logan Hess, his jaw set in a determined line, was already on the move. "Who cares? If Prescott says it's time to move, let's go."

Denver stepped into the fray, ready to lead, as always. "It's not a ploy, is it, Gray? Is that drone headed this way?"

"Not if Jerrica can help it, but maybe she can't. She's all alone with a maniac, and I let her go with him. I didn't trust her enough."

"Sounds like you trust her now and that's all

that matters." Denver charged toward the patio and the pleasant scene about to be radically altered. "Let's get these people out of here, and watch out for suspicious behavior."

Major Denver took control of the situation, ordering his team to fan out among the guests to let them know a credible threat against the party had been received.

Gray took his parents aside and told them the truth. His mother handled the situation with aplomb and grace, making light of the news with her guests but ensuring that they gathered their things and left.

Gray eased out a breath as he noticed the majority of the guests on their way out without trampling each other. He scanned the skies for an incoming drone. The security detail had been notified of the plan, but ordered not to shoot down anything or try to intercept.

Then McVie signaled him, jerking his thumb toward the house. Gray made a stop to talk to his parents. "You two need to get out of here."

His mother dug in her heels. "I'm not being driven from my home. If Jerrica thinks she can stop this thing, my money's on her."

"Dad? Talk some sense into her." Gray lifted his arms before joining McVie in the house.

What greeted his arrival in the great room caused him to trip over the track of the French doors. McVie and the others had lined up a handful of men and one woman on the large crescent-shaped sofa, a pile of cell phones and gas masks on the floor in front of them.

Sutton whistled through his teeth. "Talk about your suspicious behavior. We caught this bunch heading to the guard shack and a stash of gas masks. Convenient, huh?"

Patrick Collins, the assistant director of the CIA, aimed a polished loafer at one of the gas masks. "You'd better hold onto one of those yourself. We informed Olaf that the guests were being evacuated. He could send that drone anywhere now—a school, a hospital, a baseball game—and it's all on you."

"I could and I most certainly will."

All heads turned toward Olaf's voice, as he stepped down into the great room, Jerrica by his side.

She shot Gray a quick look from wide eyes, and then dropped her gaze to the floor.

Olaf patted the tablet he held aloft balanced on his palm. "I'll give you one more chance, lieutenant. You and your Delta Force men release my team here and nobody has to get hurt, nobody has to get gassed. But with the threat of our weapon still very much alive, we'll take control of the presidency, the government, and run things our way."

Gray shifted his gaze to Jerrica, who lifted her head and nodded once, a smile playing about her lips.

"Knock yourself out, Olaf. We have the FBI and members of the Secret Service on their way now to conduct the arrests of these individuals… and you." Gray pulled out his gun and leveled it at Olaf's head.

The man didn't even flinch. A slow smile spread across his pale face. "I don't think you want to do that, lieutenant. I already have the drone set up. Once my associate hears of these arrests, he'll know what to do."

"Let him try." Jerrica slipped the tablet from Olaf's hands.

Olaf choked. "What are you talking about, Jerrica? Y-you mean, you'd do it yourself? I can assure you, Prescott isn't going to allow that, either. He'll turn his gun on you just as easily as he did me."

"Nobody's going to do it, Olaf—not you, not me, not some shadowy associate—because it can't be done."

Olaf's face reddened, and his fellow traitors on the sofa began to murmur and shift uncomfortably.

"What have you done?" Olaf's icy blue eyes bugged out of their sockets as he turned them on Jerrica.

"You trained me well, Olaf. Now your servant is your master." Jerrica waved her hand in the air. "Did you really think I'd believe that database was so important to you if it contained just the names of the traitors? We'd learn all that information, anyway, when it wouldn't do us any good because you always had that secret weapon—the drone."

"Always had? *Have.* I have it." The veins stood out on Olaf's forehead and he wagged a shaking finger at the tablet in Jerrica's hands.

"While I was corrupting the database Amit and I uncovered, I was also using your tablet to figure out how to disable the drone." She smacked the tablet against Olaf's chest. "And I did."

Of course, Sutton was the first to hoot and holler, but the others followed suit.

Olaf sank to his knees, frantically tapping his tablet, his face getting redder and redder until it looked like that scarf was strangling him. Finally, he threw the tablet across the room and sputtered, "B-but your father. I'll rat him out. I'll turn him in. He'll spend the rest of his life in federal prison. L-look, I'll tell the FBI right now."

A swarm of dark-suited agents swarmed into the room, guns drawn, and Gray's Delta Force team gave way to them.

"Oh, well." Jerrica flicked her fingers in the air. "My father *did* break the law."

Epilogue

"Now, this is *my* kind of party." Jerrica wiggled her red-polished toes in the water as she sat on the edge of the Prescotts' pool, Gray beside her.

Martha Drake, Cam Sutton's girlfriend and the CIA translator who'd been sent the initial emails implicating Major Denver, sipped a sweating glass of iced tea. "I just can't believe Patrick Collins, the assistant director, was involved. Or, wait, maybe I can believe it. He never took our investigation seriously, did he, Cam?"

"It wasn't just Collins. We couldn't get anyone to take action. The setup against the major should've ended there." Cam scooped up some water from the pool and dribbled it on Martha's thigh.

"*You* can't believe it? How do you think I felt about that?" Sue Chandler, Hunter Mancini's fiancée and the only CIA officer present, motioned to their son on the edge of the pool. "Jump!"

"Daddy. I want Daddy."

"Of course, you do."

Hunter used his powerful stroke to swim across the pool. He patted his chest. "Right here, buddy."

"You can't jump yet." Asher Knight lowered his wriggling daughter into a plastic inner tube while his fiancée, Paige, held it steady. "Paige and I knew the plot had to go all the way to the top. They'd gotten to the doctors in rehab. I'm just sorry I played into their hands."

Paige kissed him over their daughter's head. "That wasn't your fault, Asher, and the fact you discovered what was happening, despite your injuries, helped Major Denver even more."

Cam saluted. "That's right, Asher. We only hated you for a few weeks."

"At least my fellow volunteer at the Syrian refugee camp finally debunked the story of Major Denver being involved in the bombing there." Hailey Duvall, Joe McVie's girlfriend, slipped into the pool and ducked her head beneath the water, ruining a perfect hairstyle. When she popped up, she pointed a toe at Jerrica. "If you're looking for a few reputable charities to fund with your money, Jerrica, I can give you the info."

Joe came up beneath Hailey and lifted her in the air. "Run, Jerrica. She's going to turn you into a do-gooder like her."

"What I can't believe is the traitors were actually going to use sarin on American citizens. The nuclear weapons components stashed at the embassy outpost my brother was guarding must've been decoys for Major Denver." Logan Hess's girlfriend, Lana Moreno, rubbed some suntan lotion on her mocha skin.

"Let me do that." Logan smoothed the oil on her back. "Your brother is a hero, Lana. When is that baseball field going to be dedicated to him?"

"Soon." She grabbed Logan's oily hand and kissed it. "I just hope you're not deployed when it happens."

"I'll see what I can do."

All heads turned at the sound of Major Denver's voice.

Cam waved his hand in the air. "The man finally shaved his beard and cut his hair, which actually makes you look older."

Denver threw a plastic football at Cam's head. "Watch yourself, son."

The major sat on the edge of a chaise lounge. "Did you all hear that the drone was located, thanks to Jerrica, and disarmed?"

"My father told us." Gray kissed the inside of Jerrica's wrist.

Martha pushed her glasses up the bridge of her nose. "I was happy to hear you and your fellow Dreadworm coworkers aren't going to face any charges."

"We cooperated fully and gave them evidence

against Olaf in the murder of Kiera Cramer." Jerrica shivered despite the warm sun on her bare back.

"Not to mention, you saved the country." Gray cupped her jaw with one hand.

"Hear, hear!" Major Denver raised his glass in the air, and the others followed suit.

"And our own Major Denver is not facing any charges for going AWOL." Gray raised his glass.

Sue swiveled her head left and right. "Looks like you're the only one not paired up, Rex."

"I'm good." He held up his hands. "The last thing I need right now is dates."

Denver jumped into the pool, splashing everyone and acting as a catalyst as the others followed him into the water.

As Jerrica shifted closer to the edge of the pool, Gray put a hand on her waist. "Do you know where your father is going to be imprisoned?"

"They haven't told me yet." She rubbed the end of her nose.

"I'm sorry it came to that."

"He's not. He was tired of looking over his shoulder, tired of kowtowing to Olaf. At least now I can visit him."

"Have I told you how amazing you are, hacker girl?"

"Just about a million times. It broke my heart

when I saw the look on your face when you thought I'd sided with Olaf."

"I should've known better."

"Why? I never gave you much reason to trust me."

"You gave me plenty of reasons. Except..." He smoothed his hand over her thigh.

"Except what?"

"I don't think you've told me you love me since I stumbled back into your life."

"Oh, I'll have to remedy that right now because I do—with all my heart." She leaned over and touched her lips to his ear.

Just then, Cam grabbed her ankles and pulled her into the pool. "C'mon, we're ganging up on Denver. It might be our only chance while he's still feeling indebted to us."

Jerrica rolled onto her back and pushed off the side of the pool with her feet. She tilted her head back and shouted, "I love you, Gray Prescott."

After all, she didn't have to keep her love quiet anymore.

* * * * *

*Don't miss the books in Carol Ericson's
previous military miniseries,
Red, White and Built: Pumped Up:*

Delta Force Defender
Delta Force Daddy
Delta Force Die Hard

*And be sure to check out the first two books
in her Red, White and Built:
Delta Force Deliverance miniseries:*

Enemy Infiltration
Undercover Accomplice

Available now from Harlequin Intrigue!

INTRODUCING OUR
FABULOUS NEW COVER LOOK!
COMING FEBRUARY 2020

Find your favorite series in-store, online or subscribe to the Reader Service!

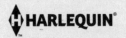

Get 4 FREE REWARDS!

We'll send you 2 FREE Books plus 2 FREE Mystery Gifts.

Harlequin® Romantic Suspense books feature heart-racing sensuality and the promise of a sweeping romance set against the backdrop of suspense.

FREE Value Over **$20**

YES! Please send me 2 FREE Harlequin® Romantic Suspense novels and my 2 FREE gifts (gifts are worth about $10 retail). After receiving them, if I don't wish to receive any more books, I can return the shipping statement marked "cancel." If I don't cancel, I will receive 4 brand-new novels every month and be billed just $4.99 per book in the U.S. or $5.74 per book in Canada. That's a savings of at least 12% off the cover price! It's quite a bargain! Shipping and handling is just 50¢ per book in the U.S. and $1.25 per book in Canada.* I understand that accepting the 2 free books and gifts places me under no obligation to buy anything. I can always return a shipment and cancel at any time. The free books and gifts are mine to keep no matter what I decide.

240/340 HDN GNMZ

Name (please print)

Address   Apt. #

City   State/Province   Zip/Postal Code

Mail to the **Reader Service:**
IN U.S.A.: P.O. Box 1341, Buffalo, NY 14240-8531
IN CANADA: P.O. Box 603, Fort Erie, Ontario L2A 5X3

Want to try 2 free books from another series! Call 1-800-873-8635 or visit www.ReaderService.com.

HRS20

Get 4 FREE REWARDS!

We'll send you 2 FREE Books plus 2 FREE Mystery Gifts.

Harlequin Presents® books feature a sensational and sophisticated world of international romance where sinfully tempting heroes ignite passion.

FREE Value Over $20

THE FORTUNES OF TEXAS COLLECTION!

Treat yourself to the rich legacy of the Fortune and Mendoza clans in this remarkable 50-book collection. This collection is packed with cowboys, tycoons and Texas-sized romances!

YES! Please send me **The Fortunes of Texas Collection** in Larger Print. This collection begins with 3 FREE books and 2 FREE gifts in the first shipment. Along with my 3 free books, I'll also get the next 4 books from The Fortunes of Texas Collection, in LARGER PRINT, which I may either return and owe nothing, or keep for the low price of $5.24 U.S./$5.89 CDN each plus $2.99 for shipping and handling per shipment*. If I decide to continue, about once a month for 8 months I will get 6 or 7 more books but will only need to pay for 4. That means 2 or 3 books in every shipment will be FREE! If I decide to keep the entire collection, I'll have paid for only 32 books because 18 books are FREE! I understand that accepting the 3 free books and gifts places me under no obligation to buy anything. I can always return a shipment and cancel at any time. My free books and gifts are mine to keep no matter what I decide.

☐ 269 HCN 4622 ☐ 469 HCN 4622

Name (please print)

Address _____ Apt. #

City _____ State/Province _____ Zip/Postal Code

Mail to the **Reader Service**:
IN U.S.A.: P.O Box 1341, Buffalo, N.Y. 14240-8531
IN CANADA: P.O. Box 603, Fort Erie, Ontario L2A 5X3